I0728454

# Jenary Stakes a Claim
### Revised Edition


By Jessie Vanderpool

Illustrated by Evan LaMarr

eta Publishing

Ocala, FL

Zeta Publishing, Inc
3850 SE 58th Ave
Ocala, FL 34480
www.zetapublishing.com

This is a work of fiction. All of the characters, names, incidents, organizations, and dialogue in this novel are either the products of the author's imagination or are used fictitiously.

Ordering Information:
Quantity sales. Special discounts are available on quantity purchases by corporations,
associations, and others. For details, contact the publisher at the address above.

Orders by U.S. trade bookstores and wholesalers. Please contact Zeta Publishing: Tel: (352) 694-2553; Fax: (352) 694-1791 or visit www.zetapublishing.com

First Published by Moose Enterprise Book & Theatre Play Publishing in 2008

Rev. Date: Aug. 2017

ISBN: 978-1-947191-28-0 (sc)

ISBN:  978-1-947191-29-7 (e)

Library of Congress Control Number: 2017950241

Printed in the United States of America

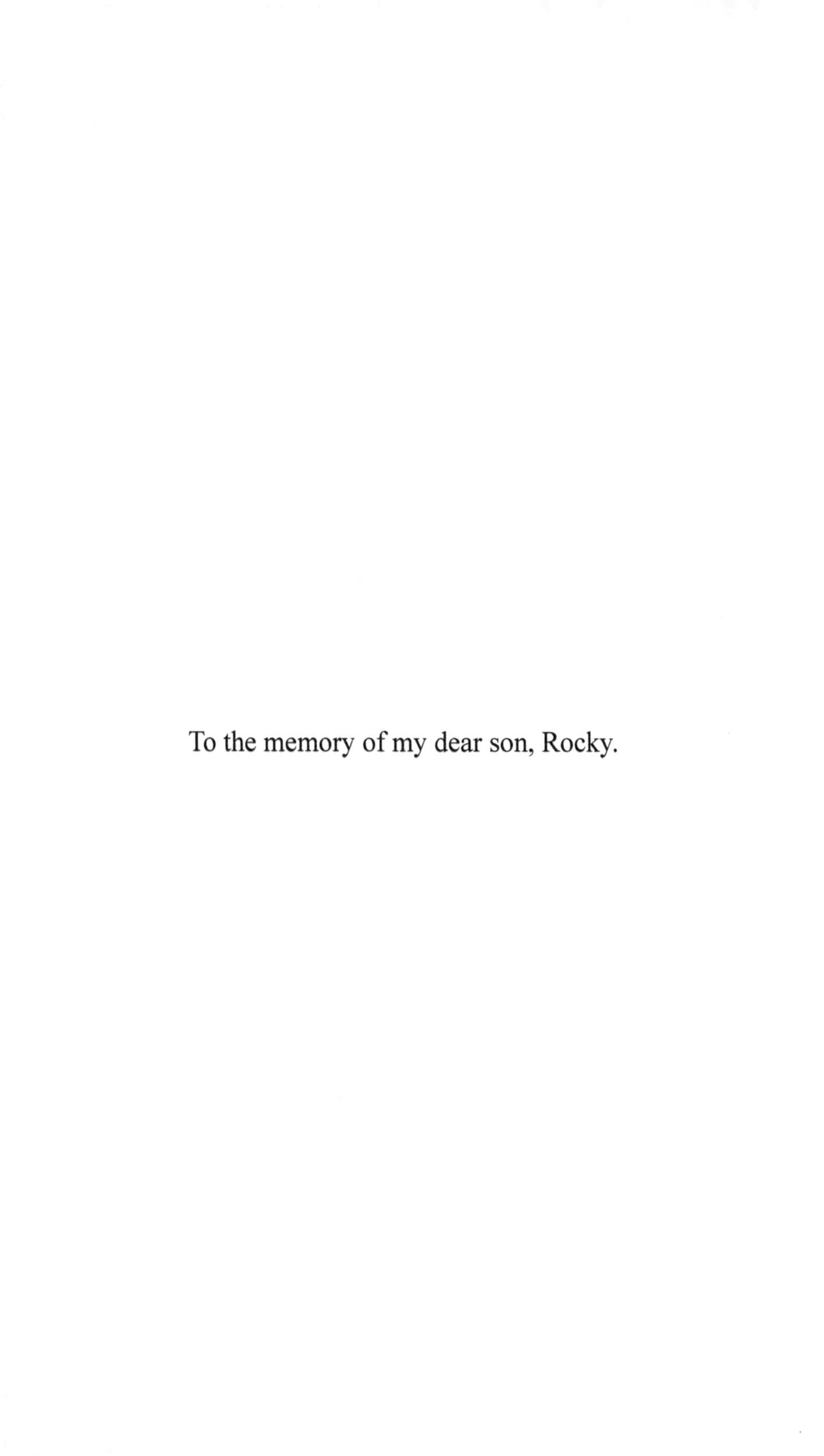

To the memory of my dear son, Rocky.

## Chapter One

September 15, 1893 was the day of the big important race. Eleven-year-old Jenny Kay Evans pushed a dark curl away from her face. Bright white moonlight flooded into the back end of the wagon. She heard the team of horses whining and set stiffly upon the quilt her mother had made for a pallet. Agitated excitement mixed with fear rushed through her body. Her stomach was turning somersaults. Sleep eluded her the previous night. She pushed a dark curl away from her face, then sat up on the pallet.

Jenary cringed when she remembered leaving home from Medicine Lodge, Kansas. She would never forget the tears in her mother's eyes when their Red River covered wagon pulled away from the only house she had lived in.

Her pa had driven this same old wagon across the barren Kansas plains. Jenary had seen farm houses and dirt rising from plowed fields as wind swept across the prairie. As they neared the border of the Oklahoma Territory, the farms disappeared. Tall grass

grass that tickled the horse's bellies stretched out across the horizon, as far as the eye could see.

A little child's cry echoed from the wagon beside the Evan's wagon. Jenary lifted the side wagon flap of heavy canvas and peeked out. Smoke drifted skyward from countless campfires. What seemed like an endless row of wagons stretched as far as she could see in either direction.

Although she did not know how long it would be before the stampede began, Jenary could barely wait for their wagon to join the others at the starting line. At exactly noon today Pa would enter this epic land rush. He planned to stake a claim for 160 acres of free land. Pa would be able to farm his own land, and never need to be a sharecropper again.

Jenary's pa, Will and her mother, Meredith were already up and warming themselves around a campfire. Smells of freshly perking coffee tickled Jenary's nose. Mother leaned over the fire, dropping dollops of biscuit dough into a big skillet of bacon fat. Jenary's mouth watered. She could already taste the biscuits covered with the sand plum jelly preserved from last summer.

Reaching over, Jenary wiggled Billy's arm. "Sleepy head, wake up," she whispered. A newly acquired mixed bred, squirming puppy poked its head out from under the quilt. A blond curl fell across Billy's eye and she brushed it back. Jenary smiled, remembering how her brother hated his 'sissy curls.' "And keep Spot quiet. Pa still doesn't know about your little dog. We'll be ready to go before long."

"Aw Sis," he grumbled, "since you've turned eleven, you're always trying to boss me!"

Jenary slipped out of her gown and pulled on her dress. She shook Billy a second time. "Mother's got breakfast fixed. Come on and get up."

"Don't step on a rattlesnake," he teased. "I heard they're worse here than back home! Some of them are even ten feet long!"

Fear crept up Jenary's spine. "Stop saying that!" She bit her lip, then carefully slipped down from the wagon. Even though she knew her brother loved to tease, Jenary could not bring herself to take another step without inspecting the ground.

Billy laughed, then scampered across the patched quilts. He pulled himself up to the seat. "I'm hungry."

"Quit playing around," Mother scolded. A wisp of dark brown hair slipped out of the knot at the nape of her neck. "We're ready to eat. Now hurry, we need to get our wagon as close as possible to the starting line."

Jenary squeezed her eyes closed and thought how much her life had changed in just two days. She remembered lying in bed, back home in Kansas, listening to her parents' whispers. She could sense the worry in Mother's voice. She knew her mother dreaded the move. Jenary had tried to stop the anxiety swirling in her stomach by squeezing her arms across it.

"It's land to be had, just for the taking," Jenary had heard her pa say. "The other lands in the Oklahoma territory have already been opened for settlement. Now they're opening up the Cherokee Strip. This is the last free land!"

"But we're doing all right here," Mother protested. "We made a good crop last fall and the children are doing well in school."

"This will be our last chance to stake a claim," Pa said, "and I plan to be right there at the front of the starting line!"

One year, Mother had planted a big kitchen garden and

Pa had put in acres of corn and wheat. Then it forgot to rain. The wheat and corn did not turn golden that summer. Pa owed more to the landowner than the crops brought at the market.

Sadness crept over Jenary when she thought about the friends she had left back in Kansas. Would she make other friends in the Oklahoma Territory? Would there even be enough people coming in for a school out here in the vast range land?

She pushed her troubled thoughts away, and walked to the back of the wagon. A lone rider on a big bay horse trotted up to their campfire. She stared at the gun slung across the fellow's horse. Jenary bit her lip. Did this stranger aim to bring danger to her family?

"Morning. I'm Blake Masters and this is King," he announced, smoothing the horse's mane.

Brown hair, with a tinge of grey clung to the collar of Pa's shirt. He stuck out his hand. "I'm Will Evans and this is the missus," he said. "Where's your wagon?"

Mr. Masters got off his horse and stepped closer. "I'm supposed to meet up with my aunt and uncle. They're going to stake a claim."

"Be good to have neighbors," Mother said.

Mr. Masters glanced at the unharnessed horses grazing on the short grass. "I'll be glad to help hitch them, Sir. That is if you could spare a cup of coffee to warm my insides."

"I'd be much obliged," Pa told him. "Help yourself to the coffee."

"I was a school teacher back in Illinois," Mr. Masters said. "My family will ship my books as soon as I get settled."

"I bet you'll be teaching my kiddoes in school," Pa suggested. "Everyone will need their younguns' help for a while though."

'Oh boy' Jenary thought, 'maybe we'll have a school afterall.'

Mr. Masters poured a cup, then sipped the hot black brew. "How did you folks know about filing a claim?"

"I heard about the government's sanctioned race for free land. There were five registration booths on the Kansas side and five south of the border, north of the Cherokee Outlet." Pa said. "About a month ago my brother, John and I came down here. I decided to put my stake on a quarter section of land close to Persimmon Creek." Pa added.

John and his family plan to settle on the other side of the creek." Pa glanced at the school teacher. "Now it's time to get the horses hitched. We need to get a good place in line."

While Jenary nibbled hungrily on a biscuit smeared with jelly, she watched as Mr. Masters stood and emptied his cup.

The school teacher patted one of the horses. "What's her name?"

"She's called Sadie," Pa said with a chuckle. "And don't give her any grief."

A smile tugged at the corner of Mr. Masters mouth. "I'll mind my manners." He grabbed a lead rope and guided the other horse to where Sadie stood. With the teacher's help, Pa hitched Prince up beside Sadie. "We're almost ready to leave."

Jenary quickly folded the quilts and sheets and tucked the night clothes under them. She closed the lid to the box of food and pushed it to the middle of the wagon.

Mother slipped her arm around Jenary's shoulder. "Keep Billy away from the front of the wagon," she warned. "We're getting ready to go and your pa will have his hands full!"

# Chapter Two

The morning breeze beat warmly against the wagon's heavy canvas. Jenary lifted the side flap and stared at the rows and rows of wagons gathered at the starting line. Carts, buggies, buck boards, chuck wagons and men on horseback were crowding among them. The horses stomped and whined restlessly.

Leaning over the wagon, Jenary looked around searching for Uncle John and Aunt Elizabeth's wagon. She hoped they were able to get a good place in line. She wondered if her seven-year-old cousin was excited.

Jenary smiled at the thought of Sarah's little brothers, Bobby Dean and Kenny Gene. She hoped to goodness that they were asleep. "Once the race begins the babies will be jarred awake.

"Yes," Mother said. "Sarah and your Aunt Elizabeth will have all she can say grace over with the little ones."

Resting on her knees, Jenary looked beyond the line and into the Oklahoma Territory. An Indian man and woman, cradling a baby stood just across the line. Jenary focused on the little boy standing beside the woman. She wondered about the family. Did the boy attend the Chilocco Mission that Jenary had heard about?

Gritty red dirt clouded the air and stung their faces as Pa pulled the horses up to the starting line. Jenary braced her hands against the rough boards of the wagon. A part of her still dreaded the rough ride to the land Pa talked about, yet Jenary felt a butterfly spark of impending excitement flutter in her tummy.

A blast of gun fire echoed, signaling the start of the race. The crowd shouted, "Oklahoma or Bust!" The race was on.

Mother held onto her bonnet as pa shouted "Yeehaw! Giddyup Sadie! Come on Prince!" His voice seemed lost, yet added to the chorus of hundreds of yelling people. Whips cracked in the air.

Excited horses lurched forward and the wagon bounced along the bumpy ground. Wagon wheels creaked and shuddered. Spring less wheels jarring the bench where her mother sat. Jenary had heard Pa tell about the open land into Oklahoma Territory. He had warned them about the deep ravines and streams, and crossing the Cimarron River. It was her and Billy's job to take care of their belongings in their wagon.

Jenary closed her eyes. For a moment she was afraid to open them. What if the wagon flipped or crashed? Would it hold together until they crossed the big River?

She pushed a strand of dark hair back from her face. The dry dust boiled up from the horses. It clogged Jenary's throat. Was all of Oklahoma territory like this. To relieve a coughing spell, she placed a handkerchief across her nose and mouth.

She glanced over at Billy holding his puppy under a pile of quilts. "Sh, sh," Billy whispered. Yet, a black tail wiggled and two dark eyes peeked out.

"Aw!. Aw!" Billy choked out, pretending to cough.

Jenary laughed. Billy was trying to cover up for his puppy. "Better keep Spot quiet," she warned her brother. "Don't let Pa hear him!"

The side wagon flap flew up, allowing Jenary to look out. Gritty dust billowed in a rolling cloud and irritated her eyes.

Leaning toward Mother, Jenary's thoughts were of Sarah's baby brothers. "I hope Kenny and Bobby don't choke on this dust."

"This is awful hard on those babies," Mother said. "Your Aunt Elizabeth draped a flour sack over the cradle. I sure hope that protects them or they will be sick."

Through red dirt, she saw the markers that the soldiers had set out before the race began. She hoped her pa remembered the exact location of their land.

Their wagon hit another big hole, Jenary bounced against the hard boards. She closed her eyes and tried not to listen to the foul shouts of the hundreds of rambunctious men. Horses galloped, stretching their legs out as far as they could reach, all trying to outrace the others.

Billy hollered. "Mother, it's taking too long. When will we get there?"

"We'll be crossing the Cimarron River real soon. Their mother clutched the wagon sides, the knuckles of her fingers turning white. "It won't be long now."       Although Jenary could hardly wait to get out of the hot dust filled wagon, she hated to complain. After all, she was not little like Billy. Mother could not change events. September was still hot and dry and the ground was so uneven.

"How much farther?" Billy asked again, impatient to get to

their destination.

"Your pa said after we cross the river, the 160 acres we hope to have would only be a few more miles away."

After what seemed forever to Jenary, Pa pulled their wagon abruptly to a stop up close to the bank of the Cimarron River. Jenary looked out. At that point, the water barely covered the sand. She turned toward her mother. "Can Pa just drive Prince and Sadie across?"

"He's going to try. It isn't the depth of the water that troubles your pa." Mother said. "The sand is really soft and may give way."

Pa jumped down off the wagon. He looked over at Mother, then sighed. He glanced back at Jenary. "We're going to have to lighten the load."

Worry rolled over and over in Jenary's tummy. She looked over at their meager belongings, the heating stove, the dishes that Mother had so carefully packed between hay, and the sewing machine.

What could they possibly set off their wagon? They could not spare any of these possessions. None of their things could be left on the river bank. "Billy and I can get out," Jenary offered. "Pa can come back for us later." She pointed to the rising cloud of dust kicked up by the bay horse and it's a rider. "That's Mr. Masters!"

The dark haired school teacher dismounted. Pa stepped forward. "What about your aunt and uncle?"

"I've already helped them cross the river. I came back for you folks"

"Could you help us set a barrel of water and the box of dishes off?" Pa asked. "We've got to hurry on!"

"Sure. Why don't I bring your children on my horse? Then I'll stay at the river." Mr. Masters said, "until you come back for your things."

Jenary held her breath as her brother eagerly jumped to the ground. "I'm out," he called. "Can I ride over with Mr. Masters, please Pa?"

"Okay," Pa said, without hesitation. "but we need to hurry."

Jenary laughed. Spot's tail wiggled out from under Billy's shirt as he ran over to Mr. Masters. She hurried after her brother.

She cringed when she saw another wagon, further down the river, stuck in the mud. Jenary said a quick prayer when Sadie and Prince dragged the wagon off the bank and into the soft river bottom. She was thankful the old team worked well together.

Her heart beat wildly when the wheels of their own wagon began to sink down to the hub of the wheels. Jenary looked back at Mr. Masters and Billy. "Do you think they can make it across?" she asked the school teacher.

"The next few minutes will tell the tale," he said, trying to sound encouraging.

Pa lean forward, urging the horses across the river, his voice hoarse from shouting and swallowing the heavy dust.

"Can we can help," Jenary asked. "If the wagon gets stuck, can we push it out?"

The teacher frowned. "We'd be swallowed up by that sand so fast that we'd pop out in China."

Jenary held her breath as Prince and Sadie struggled to pull the heavy wagon out of the silly sand. She breathed a sigh of relief when the wheels again sat on the dry ground. "Thank you, dear God," she whispered.

Billy and Mr. Masters stood beside the barrel of water and

box of her mother's precious dishes.

With the help of a new friend, Jenary and her family had come this far on their adventure into Oklahoma Territory. By sundown she hoped they would be safely home.

## Chapter Three

Speckles of bright sunlight glimmered off the water, and flashed into Jenary's eyes. It was her turn to cross. She glanced down for a moment, then clutched the saddle horn for security. She tried not to bounce up and down when King stepped into the water.

Jenary looked ahead while the horse plodded through the shallow water. She did not want to think about what might happen if King should step in a hole. What if there was quick sand in the middle of the river? Jenary sighed with relief when the horse clambered onto solid ground, then whispered, 'Thank you Lord."

Mother hurried over. "I appreciate you helping us out, Mr. Masters."

"You're mighty welcome, Ma'am," he told her, then chuckled. "Now I better go back for your boy and his puppy."

Leaning safely against her mother, Jenary watched as King carried Billy and Mr. Masters across the Cimarron River. She glanced over to where her pa stood by the wet wagon. Jenary knew

12

he was anxious to get the family to the land they had traveled so far to claim.

In the late afternoon, Pa pulled the wagon under a grove of trees, then climbed  down. Grabbing a hatchet, he pounded a stake into the ground. "Our 160 acres of land begins here," he said. "We'll need to go into Elm Grove as soon as we can and file our claim."

In a flash, Spot jumped down from the wagon. "Wait," Billy called. But the puppy darted past him and ran toward the trees.

Pa took hold of Billy's arm just as the boy began to follow the pup. "I thought I told you that we couldn't bring Spot," Pa scolded, in mock dismay "but he came anyway!"

"Spot can help us catch rabbits and squirrels. He'll be a big help to us," Billy assured Pa. "You'll see."

Stepping closer, Jenary studied her pa's eyes. How angry was he? She breathed a sigh of relief when Pa's face broke out into a big smile.

"We were able to cross the river. All of us, including Spot," Pa said. "Just see that you take good care of him."

"Oh I will!" Billy assured him. "I will!" Off he scampered with the squirming pup.

In the distance, red dirt swirled in the air. "It's Mr. Masters," Jenary called out, running toward him.

"I'd planned to turn the wagon around and come back for our belongings," Pa said.

"Uncle Fred came back for me," Mr. Masters said, sliding from the saddle. "We loaded everything into his wagon. We'll bring it over later."

Jenary danced around excitedly. She could not believe they

were really at their new home. She was beginning to like Pa's idea of free land. "Look," she said, pointing to the flourishing Oak trees. "And we have our own little creek. May I go see it?"

"Maybe you kids can go down there after supper," Mother said. She turned to the teacher. "Why don't you stay and eat with us?"

The unemployed teacher twisted the reins around his finger. "I wouldn't want to be impose," he said. "Ma'am, my friends call me Blake."

"It's our way of saying thanks for all of your help, Blake," Mother said, leaning toward the wagon's tailgate.

Mother tapped Billy on the shoulder. "Go hunt some little sticks for some little sticks so we can start a fire."

Later, Mother filled the plates with bacon, home canned beans, and cornbread fritters, then refilled their coffee cups. "Say a prayer and bless the food," she told Pa. "We want to get things cleaned up before the night sets in."

"First time eating on our new land, Mother," Jenary said. She looked over at Mr. Masters. He had been friendly. He helped unload the overloaded wagon, then carried her and Billy across the river on King. Jenary felt certain that Mr. Masters would get a school started out here, somehow.

Jenary tried to think of all the good stories Pa had told her and Billy about the opening of the Cherokee Strip and of their new home. She knew Mother tried not to cry when Pa sold almost all of the furniture. With the money, he bought lumber to repair their Red River covered wagon and two large barrels to carry water.

When they loaded the wagon back in Kansas, Pa had told Mother that they did not have room for her canned goods. Jenary was glad that her mother had stood her ground. "We may not have a nice house to live in when we reach our spot of ground in Oklahoma Territory," her mother had said, "but we won't go hungry."

"Pa, tell Mr. Masters how we picked out our very own land," Billy bragged, as Spot scampered hungrily around his feet.

Mother poured coffee into two cups. "Give one to your Pa," she told Jenary. "And one to our guest."

Jenary glanced over at Pa. Happy tears glistened in his eyes. She blinked back feelings of her happiness, glad to see Pa in such good spirits.               He and Mother came to the new land because they wanted another chance. This move would be a new start, a new beginning for the family. "Please Pa," she urged, "tell us how you first found out about the Cherokee Strip."

"Back in Medicine Lodge, Kansas, one Saturday morning. I was down at the blacksmith shop," he said. "I heard some fellows talking about free land out here in the Oklahoma Territory."

"Go on Pa," Billy urged. "Tell us what the men said."

"Hold your horses, Son." Pa laughed at Billy's impatience. "We've always worked someone else's land. We could never call the house we lived in home.

Pa took a big swig of coffee, then hurried on. "As I said before, I'd heard about the race for free land. Each person needed to register and stake a claim. We decided we wanted our own home so we came."

"The news of this free land traveled fast," Mr. Masters said. "Even back to Illinois, my neck of the woods."

"How many days away is that?" Billy asked, his eyes big with excitement.

"Two days riding day and night," Mr. Masters answered.

"Without seat padding."

Jenary laughed. Billy teased and tormented her fiercely sometimes. Yet at times like these, she felt glad he was her little brother.

Pa sipped his coffee. "A week before the starting day of the race, I obtained a permit. On this section of land close to Persimmon Creek," Pa added. "We can farm and still raise cattle."

After supper, Jenary pulled the dust-filled handkerchief out. Susanne, Jenary's best friend had embroidered a "j" on the corner of the handkerchief for Jenary's going away present. How she missed her friends back in Medicine Lodge. Would she ever see them again?

The campfire felt warm as the sun slipped below the horizon. "Tomorrow we need to go file our claim," Pa said. "Or someone else will try to take our land."

"I'll stay here with the wagon," Mother said. "We don't want anything to happen to our belongings while you're in town."

"I can come back in the morning stay and watch after things while you're gone," Blake Masters offered. "Perhaps my uncle and I will have a chance to bring over your dishes and a barrel of water."

Mother brushed a tear away. "I appreciate this," she said.

"I'd be much obliged to you," Pa told him, holding out a hand in friendship. "We can't afford to lose that water. "The missus and the children can go into Elm Grove with me."

# Chapter Four

Over the plains a bright sun peeked through the clouds. Jenary pulled on her dress and climbed down from the wagon.

Pa poured a cup of coffee to ward off the early morning chill. "We need to hurry," he said, setting the pot back onto the rocks surrounding the fire. "Every man has to file. We need to show our permit at the land office before they will recognize our claim."

"I'll wrap these warm biscuits up in a cup towel," Mother told him. "We can eat them on the way in."

Pa took a big swig of coffee. "We've come too far to take any chance on losing our land."

Mr. Masters rode out from among the trees and up to the campfire. "Good morning."

"Help yourself to the coffee," Pa said. "We appreciate you watching our land."

After they climbed into the wagon, Jenary and Billy leaned

out the back and waved to the school teacher. "Tell Spot I'll be back," Billy said.

"Giddyup Sadie and Prince," Pa called out, in a gentle voice.

Leaning back against the canvas, Jenary recalled her parents faint talking the previous evening. She was so excited to be going into town. It would be an adventure. "Oh Mother," she said. "It will be fun to see how different things are out here."

"I wish Spot could have come." Billy muttered, already missing his pup. "I bet he'll be lonesome without me."

The old wagon rocked it's way into Elm Grove. Jenary nibbled on a biscuit. Pa told her and Billy that the town was two miles south and one-half miles west from their claim. Excitement tickled every inch of Jenary. She could hardly wait to get there.

Her thoughts were interrupted when her pa told Mother about his plans. "The wagon will do for right now," he said. "We'll get started on a sod house right away while the earth is dry."

Jenary knew they could not have a big house like some of those back in Medicine Lodge, but a house made of dirt and grass. "Can't we chop down some trees and build a cabin? That will be better than living under the dirt like a ground hog."

"Maybe we can think about a frame house later," Pa said. "For now, a sod house will have to do. After all, a sod house will keep us warm this winter. Besides it will take time to dig a well," he added. "These two barrels of water won't last forever."

Jenary had never seen anything like Elm Grove. The town consisted of a plank walkway with a smattering of rough-hewn, unpainted buildings. Pa drove the wagon down the main road, banked by rows and rows of tents.

In front of the only mercantile store, the owner was

sweeping red dirt out the front door of the small building. "Mother," Jenary said, pointing to the white canvas tents. "Oklahoma Territory is sure different than Kansas."

"Yes it is, honey," Mother agreed. "Someday there will be a building in place of each tent you see."

"Right now we need to find the land office so we can file our claim," Pa said, his hands lightly slapping the reins against the team's rumps.

Jenary boldly inspected a large tent and a long line of ragged men standing in front of it. "Maybe that's the registration tent. Do we need our permit to prove where our land is located?"

Pa pulled a piece of paper out of the bib in his overalls."It's right here. Let's go over and get in line," he said. "Maybe we'll see John there."

After standing in line for twenty minutes, Jenary reached down and rubbed her tired legs. She looked over at the shade trees at the end of the street. Jenary just knew this had to be the very longest line she had ever seen. "Mother can I go sit under one of those trees?"

"Yeah," Billy grumbled, sauntering away from the line of people. "I'm hungry."

"Me too," Jenary added. Her brother seemed to always be hungry, but at this minute, she was also hungry.

Back home, Mother insisted that they do their chores and finish their lessons as soon as they came in from school. Billy always pestered Mother for a bite of food. "Where's the bucket you fixed for us this morning?" demanded the hungry boy.

"In the wagon," Mother said. "Under the quilt in the back."

Jenary and Billy walked toward the wagon. From a tent door flap, a brown skinned child emerged. "Look," Jenary exclaimed. "There's a little Indian girl. She looked to be about my age, eleven-years-old."

"I wonder where she lives," Billy said.

When they stepped toward the girl, she darted behind the tent. "I guess she's shy," Jenary said. She wanted to meet the native girl.

Jenary had just finished eating bacon and a biscuit when Pa and Ma walked toward them. "Did you get everything fixed?" she asked.

There was a wide happy smile on Pa's face. "The land is ours. Now we need is to get to work building a sod house and digging a well," he said, "then we can start farming."

When Pa drove the team onto their land, late that afternoon, Mr. Masters and Spot met them. "Does your claim belong to you folks now?"

Pa jumped to the ground, then helped Mother down. "It's ours!"

While she hung her bonnet on a tree limb, Mother glanced at Billy. "Run and get some kindling so we can start a fire, she said. "Everyone's hungry."

Mother turned, then saw a box setting under the tree. She gasped. "My dishes! My dishes! She hurried over to Mr. Masters. "Thank you," she whispered, blinking back tears of joy. "Thank you ever so much."

Pa shook the school teacher's hand. "Seems we're indebted to you again."

A tinge of red crept over Blake's face. "Uncle Fred bought over your dishes and a barrel of water. Spot and I just tagged along."

Jenary watched her mother's happiness. The dishes were

a keepsake from Jenary's grandmother. More than that, they were from back home in Kansas. She took Mother's hand. "I'm thankful they're safe."

Mother nodded. "We better hurry and get supper. Pa wants to start building the soddy early tomorrow."

"Uncle Fred brought a cutting disc from Illinois", the school teacher said.
"Perhaps I can bring that over early in the morning. That is if Uncle Fred can spare me."

"I'd be very much obliged," Pa said. "Very much obliged."

Before the sun crested the horizon the next morning, Mother and Pa drove four stakes into the ground. One at each corner where they planned to build a sod house.

Jenary watched Mr. Masters drive Prince, pulling a disc cutting the earth into strips of sod.

"Look," Jenary said. "Look what they're doing." She pointed to the men and Billy struggling to carry the thick pieces of sod.

Mother laid a cup towel over the dishes. "We need to help them move those strips or we'll still be living in this wagon when the first frost comes."

# Chapter Five

The late afternoon sun beat down warmly and Jenary brushed a strand of damp hair away from her sweaty face. She placed a sod block on the ground beside a stake. She and Mother had helped carry the long strips since early in that morning. "Can I stop for a drink?"

"Sure, honey," her mother said. "There's a cup by the barrel of water."

Jenary approached the wagon. She heard an odd scraping noise. She stooped and looked under the wagon. On the other side, she saw feet wearing a pair of Indian moccasins. Who is there? Jenary wondered.

Silently she tiptoed around the corner of the wagon. "Hello," she said to the girl who was wearing a buckskin dress. The Indian sipped water from the cup. "I remember you from town. What's your name?"

The girl pointed to her own chest. "Little Bird!"

Jenary pointed to her own chest. "My name is Jenary. Where did you come from?" she asked, softly.

Little Bird shook her head, letting dark fat braids brushed her shoulder. Looking down at her feet, she shyly backed away.

"Stay here," Jenary begged.

"Mother," she called out. "Somebody's here!"

"Who is it?" her mother asked, hurrying toward the wagon to welcome any guest.

"You can have more water," Jenary soothed. "We won't hurt you."

Little Bird stared at Jenary, then stepped behind the corner of the wagon.

Jenary gazed into her mother's eyes. "Her name is Little Bird. What should we do?"

Very slowly, Mother approached the girl. "Are you hungry, child? There's a biscuit and a piece of bacon left."

Jenary moved closer watching the Indian girl step back toward a tree. "I could pour you another cup of water."

Mother laid a cup towel on the open tail gate of the wagon. "Let's just leave the biscuit and bacon here," she suggested. "Jenary pour Little Bird some water. If we leave, perhaps she will come and eat."

Although Jenary hated the thought of turning away from the Indian girl, it would be best to try her mother's way. "I hope so."

Jenary reluctantly hurried over to piece a sod block Pa had wrestled from the earth. Quickly she carried it over to one of the stakes. "How many more," she grumbled.

"Until we get enough blocks laid," Pa said.

After laying the strip down, she looked toward the back

of the wagon. The biscuit was gone and the cup was turned over. "You were right, Mother. She did come."

Mr. Masters walked over to the wagon. "I'd better get on over to Uncle Fred's place. He may still help with the chores."

"Many thanks for all of your help," Mother said.

"When's supper?" Billy demanded, instead of asking.

"Soon. The sun's going down and it's getting cooler." Mother looked directly into his hungry stare. "Get a handful of kindling so we can start a fire."

Billy began walking away. "Be sure the sticks are little so they'll catch real fast," Mother added.

Jenary cut up seed potatoes and placed them in the pan. A good portion of the seed part would be saved for planting. Mother began fixing the squirrel that Pa had caught at daylight. "I wonder where the Indian girl went?" Jenary asked.

Mother slowly turned the skewed squirrel over the fire. The coffee pot setting at the edge of the fire, began to perk. "We didn't see any tepees close by."

"I wish she would come back," Jenary said, turning the potatoes in the skillet of bacon fat.

"What are you talking about?" Pa asked, shaking the water from his hands.        Jenary knew her pa and Billy had been down to the creek to wash their hands and splash water on their dirt-caked faces. Pa poured a cup of coffee and reclined against a log away from the fire. "We had a visitor today," she told pa.

Then Jenary began to explain , eager to be the first to relate the news of the event. Quickly she told him about Little Bird. "We don't know where she's from."

Pa sipped his coffee. "Those Indians live down south in this Oklahoma territory and over east in the Indian Territory. They need to stay to themselves and not mix with us white people."

Jenary gasped. She could not believe that her pa say such terrible words about Little Bird. "But she was hungry!"

"Let them search for food like the rest of us." Pa's voice echoed hollow and cold.

After supper, Jenary placed the dishes in the old dishpan, then laid a bar of lye soap on them. Back in Medicine Lodge, she and her family had seen Indians in town, but not very often.

Before they came to the Oklahoma territory, Jenary had heard that Oklahoma meant 'land of the red man'. Pa needed to change his thinking.

Mother placed the leftover food in a syrup bucket, then hung it on a tree limb. Pa and Billy went to feed and water Sadie and Prince and gather more wood for the morning fire.

Pouring hot water over the dishes, Jenary noticed something move. Little Bird peeked around the corner of the wagon. "Mother look here," she whispered.

Jenary blinked twice when an Indian woman and Little Bird approached the fire light. Mother stepped back. "What do they want?"

The Indian woman abruptly halted. Minutes seemed to pass. Finally the pair inched forward.

"Me Wacoma," the thin woman said.

Stepping in front of Mother, Jenary glanced at Little Bird. "Do you and your ma live around here? she asked.

The girl pointed to the darkening horizon. "Way over there. Far from home."

"Uh," the Indian mother added.

"We are too," Jenary said.

Little Bird stood very still, a tiny childish smile on redish lips.

Jenary felt happy. It had been hard for her to leave Medicine Lodge and all her friends. Maybe now Jenary can have a new friend. "I really like your name."

"Are you hungry?" Mother asked, through a throat clearing voice. "There's left over supper, and it's still warm."

"No, not ask," Wacoma said, softly. She looked down at her feet. "No."

Jenary noticed how Little Bird buckskin seemed to hang on her slender body. The little Indian girl looked longingly at the syrup bucket containing the food. "I'll get two clean plates, Mother."

"No need for anyone to go hungry," her mother said.

Wacoma said nothing, but nodded when offered the plate of food. While she watched Little Bird eat, Jenary wondered why the girl and her ma were wandering  by themselves. "Is your pa back home?"

"Now Jenary," Mother scolded. "Don't be nosey. That's none of our business."

Wacoma looked up from the plate of food. "My man leave home to find food. He not come back."

Jenary stared directly into Little Bird's eyes to see tears glistening. Jenary did not know what she would do if Pa was not here with the family. "How far did he go?"

"He say he be back before it gets really dark," Wacoma said. "But he no come home."

Mother leaned closer. "How long has he been gone?"

"Five sleeps," Wacoma whispered.

'No wonder Little Bird is hungry,' Jenary thought. She could not remember a time when there was not food to eat. Her mother and Pa always made certain that she and Billy did not go to bed on an empty stomach.

After eating a few bites of potatoes, Little Bird picked up the piece of meat. Wacoma stood, grabbing the girl's thin arm. "We go!"

"Wait," Little Bird begged.

"You can take that with you," Jenary told the girl.

Little Bird nodded happily.

"But where will you go?" Jenary asked. "Where will you stay?"

Mother slipped her arm around Jenary's shoulder. "Let them go on," she whispered. "We don't want visitors when Pa and Billy come back."

Jenary pressed her lips together angrily. If Pa saw the Indians, he would be as mad as 'an ole wet hen.' "Good-bye," she told Little Bird and offered a friendly wave.

Moments later, Little Bird and her mother vanished into the darkness.

"I hope they'll be all right," Jenary said.

"Oklahoma is their land," Mother informed her. "They'll know how to manage."

"I just hope we'll see them again. It would be nice to have Little Bird for a friend."

"I know you miss your friends back in Kansas," her mother soothed."You'll
meet new friends. Other homesteaders' children.

# Chapter Six

Moonlight filtered into the back of the wagon. Jenary glanced over at the campfire and wondered why her pa and Billy had not come.  After Little Bird and her ma left, Jenary put on her soft pink night gown. She lay down on her pallet and was almost asleep when pa's voice roared from the end of the wagon.

"Has that Indian gal been snooping around here again?" he asked Jenary.

It made her sad to think that Pa might not let her friend return. "They're gone," she told him.

Billy stepped closer. "Where do they live?"

"I'm not sure," she said. "Little Bird told me that it was a long way off. Her ma said that the pa left."

"Her ma?" Pa asked. He leaned closer. "Listen Sis," he said. "I don't want you hanging around those mean Indians."

"Little Bird isn't mean," Jenary whispered. "She was just hungry."

"Let them fend for themselves," he said, angrily. "I've got all I can do to feed my own family."

"But Pa."

"Mind what I say," Pa slapped a hand on the tail gate. "I mean it!"

Tears instantly flowed, but Jenary brushed them away. She lay back down on her pallet. Within a few minutes, Billy crawled into the wagon. He propped himself up on one elbow. "Don't cry, Sis," he whispered. "Pa will get over his mad spell."

"I've never seen him so angry," she said, softly.

"He'll be the same Pa in the morning," he assured her, "you'll see."

Jenary missed her friends something fierce. Billy was a friend sometimes, but he was also just her brother. It was not the same. There were just some things she would like to share with a girl. Jenary really liked Little Bird's buckskin dress and beaded band. She wanted Little Bird for a friend.

In the darkened morning, Jenary woke to the delicious smells of breakfast. She peeked out from the back of the wagon. Mother had cooked bacon, made drop biscuits and stood pouring the gravy into a bowl. Jenary's stomach growled.

She took off her gown and quickly pulled on a dress, then slipped her feet into shoes, without losing much body heat. Jenary climbed down from the wagon. "It smells good," she said. "I'm hungry."

Mother handed Jenary a plate. "Go ahead and fix your food, while it's hot. Pa's feeding the horses," she said. "He'll be back and ready to eat."

Carefully Jenary broke a biscuit, put two spoonfuls of gravy over it, and laid a piece of bacon on the plate. She sat down on a rock close to the campfire.

Pa walked up. "Let's hurry and eat. We want to get an early start on the sod house," he explained, accepting a cup of coffee from Mother. "Better get Billy up and moving."

Jenary swallowed the last morsel of food. She remembered how good Mother's fresh biscuits were back home. She could not wait until they were in their very own house. Even a sod house. "I'll wash the dishes," she said.

Minutes later, Billy shivered on a big rock and stared into the fire. "Why do we need to get up so early?" he complained.

Mother fixed a plate of biscuits and gravy, then handed it to Billy. "Eat so we can get started on our sod house."

By late afternoon, shadows danced against the wagon and the campsite. Jenary watched Pa place row after row of strips of sod on each side of the house. When the walls were high enough, Pa and Billy carried tree limbs to use for the roof.

Pa frowned. "I wonder why we haven't heard from John and his family by now. I hope they have their claim registered.

"I'm worried about those little ones," Mother said. "I hope they're all right."

Jenary listened to her pa and mother, then shook her head. She wanted to see Sarah and the twins too. Right now Pa needed help. "Do you need me to get more water?" Jenary asked.

"Yes honey," Mother replied, "and hurry. Your pa is thirsty and he wants to work until dark."

Jenary poured water from the barrel spout into a small syrup bucket, then reached for the long handled dipper. When she turned, jenary saw a movement. "Little Bird," she whispered. "What are you doing here?"

Without a word, the Indian girl stepped closer. Fear clawed

through Jenary. What if Pa saw her new friend? There would be trouble. Jenary knew that for certain.

"Stay here," Jenary whispered. "I need to take this water to Mother. I'll be right back."

Jenary breathed a sigh when Little Bird nodded. Walking as fast as she dared without spilling the water. Jenary arrived, set the pail down, and placed the dipper in the bucket. "Here"s the water."

"Now can you help me carry these last strips of sod?" her mother asked. "Pa's almost ready to put on the roof."

"I need to go to the privy for a minute," Jenary crossed her fingers behind her back. "I'll be right back."

"All right," Mother urged. "but hurry."

All Jenary could think of was Little Bird. Did she become frightened and leave? Could Jenary keep her friend out of Pa's sight? She walked behind the wagon, then stooped down and looked under it. "Where are you?"

Glancing toward the clump of trees, Jenary saw a brown face peek out from a gnarled one. "There you are," she whispered.

Little Bird pulled a flower from her head band and smiled. "Pretty."

"Oh yes," Jenary replied, smiling.

Laying the flower in Jenary's hand, the Indian girl stepped back. "For you."

"You brought me a flower?" Jenary asked. She blinked back a tear. She could not believe her new friend would do something so special.

Little Bird quickly ran across the brown dry grass, then stopped and beaconed to Jenary.

"You want me to follow?" Jenary asked.

"Flowers," the little Indian girl whispered.

"Yes," Jenary said, softly. "Let's go see the pretty flowers."

Little Bird moved quickly and Jenary struggled to catch up. Mother would expect Jenary to hurry back, but surely she could take time to see Little Bird's treasure. Perhaps she could bring Mother some multi-colored prairie flowers.

Running down the path, Jenary followed Little Bird to where the flowers were growing. Coming around the bend in the path, Jenary almost crashed into the vines.

Red and pink blossoms were twined around the growth along the bank of the Persimmon Creek. "Oh look," she said, softly. "Wild Morning Glories. Mother would love some of these flowers."

"Pretty," Little Bird said.

Since Jenary was a half-head tall than Little Bird, she reached up for the fully blooming flowers. Her foot slipped on the wet grass. She tried to grab a vine, but it was slippery and she fell. Her leg hit the sharp edge of river bed rock. "Help!"

"You hurt!" Little Bird cried out.

Jenary stared at the blood trickling down her leg. "Oh, It hurts!"

In a flash, Little Bird was gone. Minutes later, she returned clutching a plant. Quickly she broke off a stem and let the liquid drip onto the open wound.

Although it burned something fierce, Jenary tried not to show tears. After all she was a eleven-year-old girl. Her pa had told her so. "What's that?" she asked. "What will that plant do to my leg?"

"Make better," Little Bird said

Jenary squinted her eyes. She wanted to look down at the cut on her leg, but she was afraid. What if she could not walk back to camp?  Gathering her courage, Jenary glanced down at her leg. "Look its hardly bleeding at all."

"Me tell you," Little Bird said, smiling.

With Little Bird's help, Jenary stood. Her friend had carefully picked up a forked tree limb she had found under a nearby tree. It seemed as though the limb had been especially placed there, just for Jenary. It had grown naturally with a just-right-crook to place under her arm pit.

"Help you walk," Little Bird said.

Flowers forgotten, Jenary placed the tree limb under her arm, leaned over and took a step. With her friend's help, she limped back home. Jenary felt thankful to be back with her family

Mother stirred the beans in a big black pot while fire licked at it's side. "Where have you been?"

Jenary cringed when Pa arrived and took a vengeful step closer to Little Bird. What would he say to her little Indian friend?

"What did you do to my girl?" Pa asked.

Just as Jenary feared, Pa would think the very worst of Little Bird. "She didn't do anything wrong," Jenary argued. "It was an accident."

"Are you sure this Indian didn't cause the accident?" Pa said, with a snarl.

Jenary took a firm hold of her friend's hand. "We went to pick flowers and I slipped on some wet grass. I fell on a sharp rock."

Her mother moved the pot off the fire, then hurried over and raised Jenary's pink flowered dress to reveal a red stained leg."It's quit bleeding."

"That's because Little Bird helped me" Jenary said. "She put Indian medicine on my leg."

"What kind of doctoring is that?" Pa demanded, his face twisted with anger.

"Little Bird helped me. Please don't be mad," Jenary begged. "My leg was bleeding so badly that I couldn't walk."

"There you are, Sis," Billy called out, running up to Jenary. "We've been looking everywhere for you."

"I'm back now."

"I go," Little Bird said, backing away.

"Please stay," Jenary begged.

"Yes," Mother called. "Tell me about this medicine that helped my daughter's leg."

"Green plant," Little Bird said. She inched backwards. "I fetch. I show."

Little Bird ran down the path to the creek. A few minutes later, she returned with a plant. She offered it to Jenary.

Jenary showed the plant to her mother. "Here's the special medicine."

When Jenary turned to thank her friend, Little Bird had vanished into the evening shadows. Mr. Masters rode up on King.

"I have a surprise," he said.

"What is it?" Billy asked.

"I've been waiting for a special box to arrive in town. My books came in today. I'll be ready to start school real soon."

School. Jenary liked the classes back in Medicine Lodge. What would school be like out here in the Oklahoma territory?

"I wish Little Bird could go to school with us," Jenary said.

Mr. Masters shook his head. "Your friend will attend the Chilocco Mission for Indian children."

# Chapter Seven
## Stolen Claims


A cool breeze drifted through the window of the soddy. Pa and Billy worked on it all day. By Sundown Jenary and Mother had fixed supper and put away the dishes. She heard the clop of horse' hooves and hurried to the front door. "It's Uncle John and Aunt Elizabeth."

Pa hurried past her. "John's driving lickety split. Something's wrong!"

Mother hurried toward them. "Are the babies all right?"

Jenary rushed to the woman. She was relieved when her aunt said, "It's not the little ones."

After her uncle helped his wife down from the wagon, he set the cradle, holding the sleeping twins, and Sarah on the ground. Uncle pulled out his handkerchief out then wiped his nose. "We're not going to be your neighbors after all."

Pa placed a concerned hand on his brother's shoulder.

"Let's go inside and get a cup of coffee," he said. "I want to know exactly what happened."

Mother turned to Elizabeth. "Let's get the children inside the soddy before it gets too dark."

At the kitchen, John leaned forward. He gripped the handle on the coffee cup. "After we found our claim, I thought sure we could settle on that land."

"The land on the other side of Persimmon Creek?" Pa asked.

"Yes, but the shysters beat us there." John affirmed. By the time Elizabeth and I got to the office to register, two big fellows had already claimed the land belonged to them."

Pa sipped his coffee. "I expect the men who got your land was 'Sooners,' Pa said. "We heard they hid in ravines and tried every way to claim this land before we got here. Soldiers all the way from Camp Supply have been patrolling these claims."

Uncle John leaned across the table. "Dad gum it! Those thieves had no right to that land! It was for me and my family."

Aunt Elizabeth laid her hand on John's shoulder. "There'll be another spot for us to homestead," she assured him. "God will help us."

"Anyway," Uncle John continued. "I heard in Elm Grove that there's some land further south of here," he said. "All we can do is load our wagon and try our luck down there."

Mother glanced at Aunt Elizabeth. "You'll be too far away."

A huge hand of doom settled over Jenary's heart. Uncle John and Aunt Elizabeth had followed the rules to claim their land in the Cherokee Strip, just like Pa and Mother had done. They were not going to live just across creek. How could this happen? "We want Sarah and the babies to live closer," Jenary said, "don't we?"

"Yes we do," Mother added.

Before the sun crested the horizon, the next morning Pa and Billy along with Mother and Jenary crossed the creek. At Uncle John and Aunt Elizabeth's tent, they helped pack the wagon. Sad faces watched their wagon pull out of sight, heavy hands waved good-bye.

Jenary sat silently in the wagon heading back to their soddy. She listened to the babies crying in the distance. They did not want to leave either. Her heart was filled to overflowing with disappointment. Why did her cousins have to leave? Jenary wanted to help take care of Bobby and Kenny.

At home, Pa built a fire while Jenary peeled potatoes, then fried them in bacon grease.

"Pst, pst."

Jenary flipped the sizzling potatoes, then looked at the clump of trees behind the soddy. Black hair and a colorful headband bobbed up and down.

"Little Bird?"

The little girl inched closer. "Me here."

"I've missed you," Jenary said.

"We're going to our village," Little Bird whispered. "You remember I tell you that my father leave camp to find food?"

"Yes," Jenary answered. "Do you know what happened?"

"He got hurt. That is why he did not return. Now he comes back to us," the Indian girl explained, then slipped away.

After the supper dishes were washed and dried, Jenary pulled on her night gown. Lingering thoughts were of Little Bird. Jenary hoped the Indian family would be happy together.

Drifting off to sleep, something scurried across her bed. "Mother," Jenary screamed. Pulling herself up on the pallet, she stared into the near darkness. In the dim moonlight, she saw something small and furry on the edge of her bed.

"What's wrong," Mother asked.

"There's a mouse in my bed!" Jenary kicked at the blanket with both feet. "Get it out! Get it out!"

"That does it!" Mother announced. "Will, you've got to finish our house. We can't stay in this soddy one more night!"

"Woman I'm working as fast as I can," he muttered, sleepily. "We'll soon be in a real house."

Billy sat up. "Hey, where's the mouse?" he asked. "Spot will take care of him."

Mother pulled the blanket tightly around her neck. "Go back to sleep," she scolded.

Jenary closed anxious eyes and lay as still as possible. She knew her pa spent every spare minute working on that frame house. She and Billy helped carry boards and nails while Mother sewed curtains for the windows.

Although she hated the mouse in her bed, more than anything Jenary hated to hear her parents quarrel. She knew her pa was enthusiastic about having his own farm. Often at night they would talk softly, not wanting her and Billy to hear them argue.

By daybreak, Mother's biscuits were ready to cook while Jenary stirred the gravy. The  door burst open and Billy ran into the room. "Pa is still milking." he said.

Their mother looked over at Billy. "Why didn't you stay and help him."

"Pa's been trying to teach me to milk, but Rosie won't be still long enough for me to squeeze the milk out."

Laughing, Jenary poured the gravy into a bowl. "What did the cow do now?"

"She tried to kick over the bucket, but Pa grabbed it just in time."

A hollow knock sounded at the door and Jenary hurried to open it. Mr. Masters and an older man stood just outside.

"Is your pa home?" Mr. Masters asked, in a friendly voice.

"He's out in the lean-to milking," she said.

Smiling, Mr. Masters said. "My Uncle Fred and I will just mosey out that way."

After the men folks walked off, Mother hurried to the door. "What did the school teacher want?"

"They went to talk to Pa," Jenary said. 'What did Mr. Masters and his uncle want with her pa,' she wondered.

Billy ran out of the door and followed the men.

"You come back here!" Mother called out.

Minutes later, Pa, Mr. Masters and his uncle Fred came back to the soddy. Billy hurried behind the men with Spot prancing aimlessly beside her brother.

Mother stepped out into the yard. "I see you found him."

A huge smile brightened Pa face. "They've come to help us work on our house."

The older man held his hand out to Mother. "I'm Fred. My nephew and I want to help you get your house built. He glanced at Jenary and Billy. "You younguns can just call me Uncle Fred."

Tears caught in her eyelashes, but Mother wiped them away with the corner of her apron. "Thank you. Thank you so very much!" she said, softly. "I'll go put on a pot of coffee and fix us up a hardy meal, 'one that will stick to your ribs'."

Pa had planned and planned for the new house. He used boards cut from spruce and jack pine trees. Yet, Pa was proud when he bartered with a wagon master for a load of good smooth oak lumber to be hauled over from the trees in the Indian Territory.

For a week, Mr. Fred Masters and Mr. Masters worked with Pa. While Mr. Masters sawed the lumber, Pa carried and helped Uncle Fred nail the boards to the new frame house.

Jenary could not wait until they hammered in the last nail to close in the walls. She and her family had waited so very long to move into a new frame house.

Late Friday afternoon, Uncle Fred loaded up his tools. "We'd better get on home and get the chores done. The missus will have supper ready."

"Much obliged for all you've done to help us," Pa said. "You've been mighty good neighbors."

"We'll try to get back over here later next week." Uncle Fred told Pa. "Maybe Blake will have his intended down here by that time."

Jenary had stood back, listening to Pa and the men talk. She stepped closer to the school teacher. "What's her name?"

Mr. Masters leaned down and pulled his boot laces up tight, then whispered. "Maggie. Her name's Maggie Reynolds."

"I like her name," Jenary said. "Is Miss Maggie a school teacher, too?"

Picking up a small stick, Mr. Masters leaned against a tree. "Yes, back in Illinois Maggie taught the smaller children and I instructed the older ones."

"I bet she misses you. Who's teaching the older students since you've come down here?"

"Someone else is helping out," Mr. Masters said.

Uncle Fred stepped closer. "Blake doesn't want this fellow getting too interested in Miss Reynolds.

"Now Uncle Fred!" Mr. Masters scolded, a blush of red

creeping up his neck to his face. "You don't need to tell everything you know!"

Jenary glanced at the school teacher. She held a hand over her mouth, to hold back her school girl laughter. "When is Miss Reynolds coming?" she asked.

"In her last letter," Mr. Masters said, "Maggie said that she'd found two other families that are coming this way. Maggie's planning to ride with them."

Jenary's heart rapidly. More families were making their way to the Oklahoma Territory. She hoped they would all have children. With two teachers, school would be exciting. It would not be long now before the ding of a school bell would be welcoming tardy children.

# Chapter Eight
## The Fire

Through the fall's crisp breeze, leaves drifted to the dry grass around the soddy. In the distance the new frame house stood. Pa told Mother that he hoped to add a front porch before they moved into their new home.

Jenary and Billy had slept on pallets since the family arrived in the territory. Somehow, Pa managed to trade for several iron bed frames. Afterwards her mother and pa took the thick canvas off the wagon. Mother cut and sewed the coverings on her treadle sewing machine, then filled them with hay to make mattresses.

While she smoothed out the feed sack sheet, Jenary remembered the one rainy day she had helped her mother. Together they sewed four feed sacks together for the sheets and two for the pillow slips.

Smiling, Jenary placed the pillow up against the iron head

board, then laid the quilt on top. She often wondered what Pa had traded for their beds. Nevertheless, she and Billy were grateful. Mattresses of hay were sure better than sleeping on a pallet.

Earlier in the morning, her pa had told Jenary and Billy that he needed some supplies for the frame house. He and Mother planned a trip into Elm Grove.

"We won't be gone long." Mother took off her apron. "After you finish making up the beds, will you please wash the dishes?" She reached for her pocket book. "Don't forget to sweep the floor."

"I won't," Jenary assured her. "I'll do it just like you showed me. What do you want me to do after that?"

"Tomorrow is wash day," Mother said. "You need to gather up all of the clothes, then sort them out. Don't forget the cup towels."

"All right," Jenary agreed. "I'll get everything ready."

"And have Billy carry in some wood. Tell him to lay it by the wash pot so we can build a fire bright and early."

"I'll tend to it," Jenary assured her mother.

Mother walked toward the door, then turned around. "There's some left over beans and cornbread. You and Billy can eat them if you get hungry before we get home."

"We'll be all right," Jenary told her.

Her mother laid her arm on Jenary's shoulder. "I'm sure you will. You're a good girl and a big help to me."

Pa helped Mother get into the wagon, then climbed up and sat beside her. "Now, Son, you help your sister," Pa said, shaking a warning finger Billy. "And don't be tormenting her. You've got to work together."

"Yes sir," Billy said, while a playful pup ran around his feet barking.

Jenary waved good-bye. The wagon disappeared over the hill. "Let's get finished," she said. "Work before play. Won't Mother and Pa be surprised when they come home to find that we did every task they ask of us?"

Billy threw a stick as far as possible. His little dog chased after it madly. "Spot and I want to play for a while."

"After we get everything done," Jenary said.

"Aw Sis," he grumbled. "Work, work, work. You're too bossy. When can we go down to the creek?"

"Do you want Mother and Pa to come home before we finish our chores?"

Billy dug his toe into the dirt. "I guess not," he whispered.

Jenary realized that she needed to get her brother into a better mood. "I bet I can get the dishes washed and the floor swept before you can bring in the wood," she said, challenging him.

Billy sprinted out toward the grove of trees. "Bet you can't!" Spot barked, following closely on Billy's heels.

Smiling, Jenary pulled the breakfast dishes out of the hot soapy water. She poured water from the tea kettle over them, then turned the dishes over on a cup towel to dry. Mother worked so hard, it seemed that she was busy every minute of the day. Jenary wanted to do something more to help.

She ran to the door and grabbed the broom. Billy had carried small limbs from the fallen trees and stacked them beside the black wash pot. Sometimes Billy grumbled, but Jenary was proud of her little brother.

Billy puffed out his chest. "Come and look!" he called out.

Jenary looked over at the big pile of wood. "You did good!" she said. "Just like Pa showed you."

Jenary had seen her pa start a fire and had helped Mother put the clothes into the boiling water. Pa had cut the handle off an old worn out broom and Mother used that to stir the wash. Could Jenary and Billy make a fire and wash the clothes?

"Come and help me," she said. "Let's start a fire and wash the clothes today. Then tomorrow we'll have more play time."

"No. We don't know how to do that."

"Yes we can do the washing," she insisted. "You can help me wring the water out of Pa's overalls. We can have the clothes hung up to dry before the folks get back from town."

Billy reached over and patted Spot. "We want to go play now."

The puppy barked eagerly.

"Come on," Jenary said. "Help me draw the water and fill the pot. You can play later."

"All right," he muttered.

With Billy's help, Jenary filled the wash pot with water. "That's full enough," she said. "We don't want the water to splash out."

Kneeling down, Billy carefully pushed the small limbs under the pot. He added larger pieces of wood. "It's all set."

"Now you can light it," she said. "Get the kindling started first."

"I know how to make a fire," Billy said, proudly. "Pa showed me how."

When the water began to boil, Jenary added the towels and wash rags, then put in the pillow cases. She grabbed the cut-off broom handle. Carefully she pulled it through the water. "Mother's going to be really proud of us!" Jenary boasted, her voice filled with excitement. Wouldn't their mother be surprised?

Jenary wrung the water out each item and rinsed them in the cool clean water. She draped the wash over the plum bushes to dry. She dropped Pa's overalls into the black wash pot and swished them around with the short stick.

She glanced over at Billy and laughed at spot ran along beside her brother. A wave of thankfulness sweep over Jenary. She could not have started the wash without her Billy's help.

There was only a slight cool breeze earlier when Jenary began the washing. Suddenly a big gust of wind blew across the yard, fanning the fire. "No! No!" she cried out.

The fire grew taller and sparks jumped and landed in a pile of leaves. Jenary sucked in her breath. This could not be happening. "Oh please! No!"

The spark ignited and the flame grew bigger. "Help," Jenary called. "Help."

"Fire!" Billy shouted, running toward her.

She gazed at the fire growing taller and wider. "Where are the buckets? Get some water! And hurry!" Jenary called. "The fire is headed toward the soddy!"

'Oh please, don't let it get to the frame house', she prayed, silently.

"I'll get the bucket, Billy said. "They're on the wash bench."

"Don't get too close to the fire!" she cautioned.

Jenary looked up. The flames rushed through the dry grass! She had to stop the fire from spreading! She coughed. Through the smoke, she could see the fire inching by yards toward the new home!

Pa had worked so hard. With the Masters and the rest of the family's help, he had nearly finished the house like Mother wanted.

Now the terrible fire was threatening to destroy it. Jenary's eyes watered. Her throat burned, yet she grabbed hands full of sand and threw it at the fire. Out of the corner of her eye, Jenary saw Billy running from the creek, clutching the bucket.

Water sloshed out of the nearly-full pail that Billy dragged along the path, soaking his pant's leg.

Jenary ran to her brother. She glanced at the tears in Billy's eyes, then grabbed the bucket of water. She poured the cold liquid on the flame. "You did good," she said. "You helped save the soddy."

With Billy's help, Jenary threw more dirt on the fire. Yet it burned on. What could she do? She could not allow the flames to touch their new house. She looked down into the wash pot. Why had she not thought of this before?

She grabbed the bucket and dipped it into the water. "Help me get the water out!" she called.

"But, it's hot!" Billy said.

"Get the other bucket. And hurry!" Jenary called out. Quickly, she filled the pail, threw it on the blaze, then dipped into the big black pot again.

"It won't go out!" Billy cried.

Spot cowered under the plow at the edge of the path leading to the out house.

She knew that her brother was right. Jenary ran to the wash pot for more water. "Pa's overalls!" she shouted. "I saw him beat out a fire with a wet gunny sack," she told Billy. "We'll use his britches!"

"Pa will tan our hide!"

"Quit arguing!" Jenary scolded. "Help me get these out of the pot."

Billy stretched up on one foot, then the other. "Do you think it will work?"

"We've got to try something," she told him.

Jenary tugged at one leg of the heavy, wet overalls while her brother pulled on the other leg.

"Ugh!" Billy grumbled.

Moments later, Pa's overalls popped free of the water. "There," Jenary said, grabbing the bib.

Holding the heavy wet britches between them, they hit the fire again and again.

"Is it out?" Billy asked.

Wiping a wet, smoky hand across her face, Jenary said. "I think so."

She glanced over at her brother. Black dirt streaked his face and soot circled one of his eyes like a racoon's mask. Billy and Spot looked almost alike. Jenary knew she could not have stopped the big fire if it had not been for her brother's help.

"There," she said, looking off in the distance at the dust billowing up into the sky. "Mother and Pa are coming back."

Jenary grabbed Billy's hand. "I hope they won't be mad at us."

Billy jerked away from her. "I wonder what they brought home?"

"Don't ask for any candy," she cautioned. "You know Pa and Mother have put everything into the house."

"Whoa, Sadie. Whoa, Prince," Pa called out to the horses.

He pulled hard on the reins, then jumped down from the wagon. Pa reached out his hand and helped Mother down. "What happened? We could see smoke arising in the wind."

"There was a fire," Billy announced, his words tumbling

over and over, "but we put it out."

Mother walked over to the soddy and looked inside.

Jenary cringed. What would mother say? So far Pa had not scolded them. "It didn't get inside," she said.

Mother pulled Jenary closer and hugged her. "I'm just thankful neither one of you were burned.

"We tried to help," Jenary told her mother, "to save you time so you wouldn't have to do all the washing."

Looking over at the frame house, standing so proudly on the hill, Jenary said, "And the fire didn't even get close to our new house."

"Look at my overalls!" Pa grumbled. "There's a big hole in the seat."

"I can sew a patch on them," Mother said, laughing. "The main thing is that our children are safe."

With the back of her hand, Jenary brushed at her dark tear streaked eyes. She knew her mother had dragged her feet about leaving their old home in Kansas. Everything was going to be all right. She just knew it would be.

After supper, Jenary pulled on her gown and lay down in a new metal bed. She shivered and pulled the thin quilt up to her neck.

She was ever so glad that the fire had not burned their new house. Jenary felt grateful that Mother and Pa were not angry at her and Billy. Most of all, she was thankful that they would be happy in their new home in Oklahoma Territory.

But what of Little Bird? Would Jenary ever see her again? And it was not fair that Uncle John and Aunt Elizabeth lost their claim. Jenary hoped that they would find a good home.

Would Miss Reynolds travel all the way from Illinois to

marry Mr. Masters?

Jenary's thoughts raced. What adventures lay ahead of her while she grew up on a homestead in Oklahoma Territory?

*Part II*
*Chapter One*
*THE TORNADO: 1894*

Angry March winds in the Oklahoma Territory blew through the leaf buds of the Elm and Oak trees. Twelve-year-old Jenary Kay Evans pulled the ties of her bonnet tighter while looking out across the homestead's buffalo grass pasture.

Late in the afternoon, Pa had asked her to bring the lone cow to the barn. Glancing up at the lowering grey sky, Jenary knew Pa wanted to be out of the wind while milking Nellie.

Jenary liked the coolness and the smell of the hay in the barn. Pa had swapped out labor with Mr. Masters' uncle Fred and they built a barn on each other's place. Pa's barn was for their horses, Prince and Sadie, and an attached lean-to shelter for Nellie, the Guernsey cow.

Jenary glanced up at black ominous clouds hovering overhead, erupting higher and higher, shooting out bolts of lightning. Thunder rolled across the prairie. She hoped that her brother was with Pa. Perhaps he was already home.

Jenary gazed out across the pasture. "Where is Nellie?" The wind jerked at the strings of her bonnet. 'Drat it! Our cow's just drawling along' she thought. 'There's nothing to do but go bring the slow poke home'.

Hurrying across the pasture, Jenary called, "Here Nellie. Come on!"

A sprinkle fell on her hand. She hoped the rain would hold off until the cow got home. "Yeah! Hurry Nellie! Yeah!" To Jenary's relief, Nellie headed toward the barn. Quickly she opened the gate and Nellie mooed! "Good girl," Jenary said.

Another clap of thunder rumbled across the heavens. Jenary trembled, then dashed for the house. The door opened and her mother stepped out onto the front porch.

Mother  took a firm hold on Jenary's arm and glanced up at the dark clouds. "A storm is coming. Pa's putting the horses in the barn."

Soon, Pa came running from around the side of the house. "A funnel's in those clouds. We've got to get to the cellar!"

Billy dawdled along to the porch. His black and white mixed breed dog, Spot, trailed behind him.

Mother grabbed the boy's arm. "Quit poking along! A bad storm is coming! Run to the cellar! Hurry!"

He jerked from her grasp. "You're such an ole scaredy cat!"

"I'll make you think 'scaredy cat'. Quit playing around!"

Pa snagged a lantern off the porch and ran across the back yard.  He struggled to hold the cellar door open in the increasing wind.  It churned clouds of dirt. Mother's big round wash tub spun across the yard.

Jenary, Billy and Mother hurried down the steps. Pa leaped to the bottom step and let the door slam. "We're safe now."

Dark shadows hovered in the corners of the underground room. Jenary could barely see the shelves, filled with Mother's canned fruits and vegetables.

In the dim light, her mother reached for a box of matches to light the lantern. "Now we can see a little better."

"Woof! Woof!"

"Spot," Billy called out. "He's still outside!"

"It's too late," Pa said. "That dog will just have to take his chances."

"Please Pa," Billy begged. "Please!"

Jenary heard the panic in her brother's voice and saw his eyes blink rapidly. He tried not to cry. "Can't you open the door just a tiny bit?"

Without a rebuttal, Pa lifted the cellar door slightly. A gust of wind showered everyone with dirt. The little dog squeezed in, scampered down the steps, then jumped into Billy's anxious arms.

Billy sniffed, then wiped his nose with the back of his hand. "Thanks Pa."

A roaring wind howled and beat against the wide heavy plank door. Jenary twisted the corner of her apron. "Do you think our new house is still standing?"

"There's no telling," Mother whispered. "We need to pray. We need to pray real hard."

Heavy objects assaulted the cellar door. Jenary watched the door bounce up and down as if hands were trying to open it. Muscles corded in Pa's arms, his knuckles whitened as he gripped the door's rope handle. Beads of sweat gathered on his forehead. Jenary saw the worry in Pa's brown eyes. In her heart, she knew that he would do his best to keep the door shut.

She remembered the tornados back in Kansas. She had seen huge Oak and Elm trees pulled up by their roots. A barn was blown completely down on a neighbor's farm.

She closed her eyes for what seemed like an hour. It had only been minutes when Mother shook her. "The wind's stopped. Pa's going to open the cellar door."

Jenary's heart pulsed in her throat. 'Please dear Lord,' she prayed silently, 'don't let our home be destroyed'.

Pa hurried up the steps and pushed the door open. Jenary followed close behind.  She ran across the back yard. "Look at the wagon!" she called out. It lay upside down. "The wheels are still turning."

"The roof on the chicken house is gone," Pa added.

Billy followed with Spot at his heels. Awe filled his voice. "What happened to the trees? It looks like they were scalped."

Jenary bit her lip. She did not want to laugh, but the Oak and Elm trees did look peculiar. They had no sprouting leaves. "The main thing is that our house is still here!"

"Thank God," Mother whispered.

Boards from Nellie's lean-to shelter lay scattered across the yard, along with pieces of the barn's roof. Jenary and her family spent the rest of the afternoon gathering the usable lumber, stacking it inside the barn.

The pieces of splintered wood, Jenary carried to the kindling pile. On the prairie in this Oklahoma Territory, no wood could be wasted.

Later, Jenary helped Mother fix a supper of fried potatoes and collard greens. A pan of golden corn bread baked in the oven while Pa tended to the spooked animals.

With the events of the afternoon continuing to replay in her mind, Jenary poured hot water into the dish pan, then put the dishes into the soapy water.

Mother lit the evening coal oil lamp, then called, "Billy, come help dry the dishes."

"Aw, Ma, do I have to tonight?"

"Yes," Mother told him. "We're all tired. Hurry before it gets too dark . . . ."She was interrupted by a knock on the door. Mother hurried to answer it. "Lord have mercy!" she called back. "Look who's come! John and Elizabeth, and their children!"

"The babies are here!" Jenary said. The storm as well as the dishes were forgotten. She dashed to the front room. With their brown wavy hair and blue eyes, Jenary thought the twins were precious. "They look just like each other!"

"Did a cyclone come through here?" John asked. "How much damage did it do?"

Pa rose from his chair. He chuckled. "Nope, wasn't a tornado, just an afternoon breeze." Then on a more serious note, he added, "We're very thankful that our house and barn were left standing."

"We saw the black cloud," Uncle John explained, "and slowed down. We were afraid we'd run right into the storm."

"The cloud came up pretty fast." Pa retold the day's events. "This morning the wind blew from the south, but before long it changed. Seems like the wind blows all of the time here."

"It sure does," John agreed, "but I'm glad it didn't tear up your place too bad."

"The big wind made everything go up in the sky," Sarah said.

Jenary glanced down at her younger cousin and reached for

her hand. "Look how big you are! And your baby brothers are so sweet."

"Hi," Sarah whispered, moving closer. "My brothers can roll over and everything."

Pa motioned toward the pot of coffee on the stove, then asked. "How are things down south?"

John poured a cup, then leaned forward. "We found an abandoned claim about ten to twelve miles this side of the Canadian River."

"Was the claim the full 160 acres?" Pa asked.

"Yes. And it has been good farm land," John affirmed.

Mother walked up behind Pa and laid her arm on his shoulder. "Why do you suppose those folks abandoned their place?"

Aunt Elizabeth, with Bobby in her arms, rocked from side to side. "The people in town told us that the wife got really bad sick. With two little children, the husband couldn't take it anymore. He went back to Kansas to be near his folks."

"Anyway," Uncle John continued, "we hated to leave this part of the country, but we were mighty grateful that we had a good warm soddy last winter."

"We were awful worried when you lost your first claim," Mother said, "but we're thankful you found another good piece of land."

Elizabeth patted the baby. "I told you that God would help us find another place to live. And He did."

Mother placed the coffee pot back on the stove. "Everything seems to have worked out for the best," Mother said. "We're just glad you've come for a visit."

"We want Sarah and the babies to stay a long time, don't

we?" Jenary said, bouncing Kenny on her knee.

# Chapter Two
## Billy and The Creek

Jenary pushed open the screen door, and stepped onto the back porch to welcome a bright new morning. She was filled with hope of happier days for herself and her family in this Oklahoma Territory. They had survived the tornado.

Fluffy white clouds drifted lazily high above. A south wind with hints of summer, whipped around the corner of the house, pulling at Jenary's pink gingham apron. She hoped it did not blow away Pa's young crops.

She turned and gazed back into the kitchen. Her cousin Sarah leaned against her pa's knee. 'My how she has grown', Jenary thought. Sarah was a year younger than Billy, but Jenary figured that if they stood side by side, they would be about the same height.

In the corner of the room, sleeping on a folded quilt, were the babies. Jenary stepped closer to Kenny and Bobby. She recalled when Sarah and her folks lived in Kansas.

Mother had looked after Sarah when Aunt Elizabeth and Uncle John's baby, Tommy, died. No one enjoyed the red birds or Christmas that year.

All winter, Jenary and Billy had played with Sarah. Sometimes Sarah spent the night at Jenary's house. Not a day went by when Aunt Elizabeth did not cry for her lost baby.

One night, Jenary overheard Pa and Uncle John whispering outside the open bedroom window.

"I don't know what I'm going to do about Elizabeth," Uncle John said, sorrowfully. "If she doesn't snap out of this, I'm afraid I'm going to lose her too."

Jenary leaned closer to the window sill. Pa said, "What about you and Elizabeth following us to the Oklahoma Territory?"

"I don't know," Uncle John whispered, his head swaying heavily. "Some days she sits and stares out the window. I can't even get her to talk to me, much less agree to anything. I miss our baby boy something fierce, but we've got to keep going someway."

"This is the race of all land claiming races," Pa said. "They're opening the Cherokee Strip for settlement. The way I hear it folks are coming from all the states around to make a new start in the Oklahoma Territory.

"Among the honest people are the land speculators. Those money-grabbing shysters aim to buy the land and sell it at a higher price. If that happens, folks like us won't ever be able to file a claim on any land.

"The ones in charge keep changing the date to keep out those thieves. I try to keep my ears open to what's going on, but I'm not certain when they'll set the date for the race," Pa said, "meanwhile, it will give you time to persuade Elizabeth to start over."

Jenary knew that Pa attempted to keep things ready. Mother packed and repacked the boxes of dishes every evening; Pa talked about loading the wagon and driving Prince and Sadie toward the Oklahoma Territory.

While Mother and Pa waited to hear the exact date of the race, Jenary heard her folks talking. Soon Sarah would have a baby brother or sister. Over the passing months, Jenary watched Pa help Uncle John sell their furniture, buy and outfit a wagon.

Little did Aunt Elizabeth and Uncle John know they would be blessed with twin boys. The new babies would help heal the terrible hurt in Aunt Elizabeth's heart. John lovingly built cradles for Kenny and Bobby. They were ready for the land race into Oklahoma Territory.

By the time the babies were three months old, the final date for the race had been announced. Although Uncle John and Aunt Elizabeth lost their first claim, God had blessed them with another fair piece of land.

Jenary glanced at the trees in the grove past the barn. Although she had been thankful that their house and barn were left standing, she had not noticed those fallen trees. How many had the tornado torn up? Maybe there were more uprooted trees further out. Perhaps more were destroyed along the trail to the creek.

Jenary walked back into the house. She reached for Sarah's hand. "Want to go down to the creek?"

"Yeah!"

Crouching down beside Pa, Billy jumped to his feet with excitement. "Spot and I want to go, too!"

Pa turned in his chair. "Son, you go with the girls and watch after them."

Billy puffed out his chest. "All right, Pa," he said. "I'll look after them."

Jenary turned her head to hide a smile. Billy was three years younger than herself, yet he was proud that Pa had given him so much responsibility.

Skipping down the trail to Persimmon Creek, Jenary took Sarah's hand. Her cousin was excited to be on an adventure. Nearing the creek, Jenary heard the rumble of the rushing stream.

"Listen," she said, "You can hear the water."

Billy ran down the path with Spot racing along side. "It's really full. Come and see!"

"It must have rained a lot during the tornado," Jenary said, explaining. "Let's hurry."

"I want to see the water!" Sarah called out.

In spite of the fallen trees, Jenary thought the pink and red wild flowers growing around the stumps were pretty.

Spot ran back and forth, excitedly. "Woof!"

"Look how deep it is!" Billy shouted.

Jenary tugged at her cousin's hand. "Let's hurry!" she urged.

"Billy's already beat us," Sarah said. "We can run."

Jenary hurried down the trail. Wild water stained with reddish-brown from silt, rushed down the swollen creek. "I can't even see the bottom."

"It's too muddy!" Sarah added.

Billy called out, as he stepped closer to the slippery bank, "It's almost full to the brim."

"Don't get too close," Jenary cautioned.

"Look there's a whole tree floating down the creek," Billy hollered. "It don't have any leaves on it!"

"It doesn't have any leaves," Jenary corrected.

"Woof!" the little dog barked as it scampered along the bank.

"Spot wants to play on the log," Billy hollered. "Come back Spot! Come back!"

Before Jenary could stop her brother, he too ran along the creek, chasing Spot. She rushed after them. "Billy you're going to fall in!"

Her heart seemed to jump into her throat when the dog leaped into the water. "Let Spot go!"

Billy inched even closer and looked down into the swirling muddy water. "It's too deep! Spot will drown!"

Jenary raced after her brother. "The dog will be all right. He can swim. You're the one who doesn't know how to swim real good. He's not going . . . ."

Billy's feet slid even closer to the swirling creek water. He flung his arms out, reaching for a bush or limb along the bank. "Help!" he cried out. "I can't stop!"

Jenary screamed. She grabbed Sarah's hand and dashed along the bank. "Billy!"

She stumbled over the sticks and bigger branches. "Grab hold of something!" she called out.

Billy shouted, but Jenary could not hear the words. He disappeared into the turbulent murky water.

Jenary froze. Had their promise of a new beginning in the Oklahoma Territory ended in tragedy? Would they lose Billy like Uncle John and Aunt Elizabeth had lost their little baby, Tommy? Jenary could not allow this to happen!

# Chapter Three
## Saving Billy

Jenary stared at the swirls, frantically searching for Billy, hoping that he would bob to the surface. Yet, the on-rushing water carried him down the creek. It seemed as if he was moving faster and faster. What if he drifted further away from the bank?

She stared at the small limbs and large branches. What if the debris pulled Billy into the whirlpool, swallowing him? Could he get loose? What if a limb hit him on the head and knocked her brother unconscious?

Worry shot through Jenary's mind. She called back to Sarah. "Run back to the house. Get Pa!"

"Help!" Billy shouted, bobbing up and down.

Frantically, Jenary watched her brother tumbling in the bubbling water. Spot climbed out onto the bank, then shook muddy droplets of water all over Jenary's clean dress.

"We'll get him out, Spot!"

'What to do? Think, Think'. Jenary's thoughts tumbled over and over. She wracked her brain. What had Pa taught her to do? 'Never jump into the water to save someone for they might drag you underneath'.

But this was her brother! Could Jenary save Billy or would they both drown? She needed to do something. Now! If only she had a rope! Anything that Billy could grasp!

Slipping and sliding down the bank of the creek, Jenary tried to keep up with him. She looked frantically for a long stick. She stumbled over a long sturdy limb.

Snatching up the branch, she held it over the water. "Grab hold!" she shouted. "Billy look up. Grab hold before you go under!"

Billy spit out a mouth of water. "I can't reach it!" he shouted.

"Drat it! This thing's too short!" She could not reach Billy. She flung the stick away, angrily. She had to find a longer branch! Jenary wondered if she could stick a limb into the ground? Would it hold? Could she lean out far enough to reach him?

Jenary breathed a quick prayer of thanks when she saw her brother clinging to a bunch of debris. Searching, she found a small sapling leaning over by the water's edge. She pushed and pushed, then brought her heel down hard and stomped with all of her might. Finally the trunk snapped. "I've got one!"

Dashing along the bank, Jenary reached the spot where Billy struggled to keep his head above the foamy dirty water. Getting down on her knees, she held the sapling far out over the water and shouted. "Now grab hold!"

The sapling was heavier than she had imagined. It seemed almost impossible to hold. Jenary laid on her stomach, dug her elbows into the wet dirt, and held on tightly.

The sight of Billy's lifeless body flashed into her mind. She pushed the thought aside. She could not allow her fears to invade her heart. She hoped against all odds that Billy could reach the sapling. Jenary held her breath when he raised up out of the water.

Billy stretched out as far as he could. "I touched it," he called out, then the current sucked him into a whirlpool of leaves and twigs. He struggled to keep his head above water while he thrashed about. "Move it a little closer!"

Inching forward, Jenary reached the edge of the bank. She took a deep breath and leaned over the water. "Quick, grab hold before I fall in too!"

"I got it!" Billy shouted. "Pull me out!"

Pulling as hard as she possibly could, Jenary struggled to her feet. She needed to get Billy out. A little bit more.

Suddenly strong hands gripped the branch and pulled hard, bringing Billy to the edge of the creek and to the bank.

Jenary turned and collapsed against her pa's chest. "Thank you," she whispered. "I was so scared!"

"You did good, girl. You did real good," he said, "and it was smart to send Sarah for help."

Pa dropped the limb and embraced Billy. He threw an old quilt around her brother's shoulder. "Thank God you're safe!"

Blinking back tears of happiness, Jenary glanced over to see Uncle John frown at Billy, then at Spot. "You've got to learn to swim!" he admonished, "like this dog did. But jumping into that swollen muddy creek is not the way!"

Pa nodded. "Right now we had better get back to the house and get this boy into some dry clothes before his mother skins us all alive."

Excited now that the horrible event was over, Billy talked non-stop about his adventure. Jenary listened and prayed that her brother would not attempt that feat again.

A supper of fried squirrel, with biscuits and gravy, smelled delicious. Jenary attempted to eat a bite or two of everything, but her eyes would not stay open. After running along the creek bank and worrying about Billy, Jenary was exhausted. "I'm too sleepy to eat," she whispered.

"Go on to bed," Mother encouraged. "We'll save some and you can eat later."

Almost asleep, Jenary lay down on her bed and closed heavy eyes. The scene at the creek replayed in her thoughts. Billy floating in that dirty water! Jenary held out the branch as far as she could, but she could not reach Billy. He floated down the stream faster and faster, farther and farther away from her. "No!" she screamed. "No!"

Mother shook Jenary lightly. "Wake up, honey!"

Jenary awoke and brushed at teary eyes. "It was awful! Billy drifted down the river and drowned!" she cried. "He drowned!"

Mother sat on the edge of the bed, slipped a comforting arm around Jenary, and held her close. "I know it was scary, but your brother's all right. It was just a dream."

Jenary wanted to believe her mother, but memories of the frightening episode lingered. "Are you sure?" she asked.

Mother Evans smiled. "Yes, Billy's all right because you saved him." She touched the scratches on Jenary's arm. "Let me put some salve o those."

"Where's Sarah?" Jenary asked. "Was she real scared?"

"She was shaking like a leaf," Mother said. "She was too

shook up to go back to the creek with Uncle John and Pa, but she's just fine now.  Why don't you get up now and try to eat a bite."

While Jenary ate supper, Sarah sat beside her. "I brought my doll, Sally," she told Jenary. "See the red dress that Ma sewed for my doll? Isn't it pretty? Maybe we can play together later."

After such a nightmare, Jenary did not know if she felt like playing with her doll, Helen. Yet Sarah wanted to play, so Jenary would do it for her.

Sarah would probably want to sleep real close to Jenary that night so she would not be scared. That would be all right with Jenary.

She had wanted to come to the Oklahoma Territory. But, after the day's events, she wondered about the hope of good times this land had promised. Jenary had been so afraid for Billy. She did not want any more nightmares!

## Chapter Four
### Mr. Masters' Plans

A healing morning sunshine poured through the kitchen window. Sarah nibbled on a piece of bacon. Jenary glanced at Aunt Elizabeth. "Why can't Sarah stay another day?"

"Yeah!" Billy added, his mouth crammed full of biscuits and gravy. "We don't want Kenny and Bobby to leave either."

Uncle John stood hovering over the table. "We need to get on home," he explained. "A neighbor fed the chickens and milked our cow for us. We let them keep the milk and eggs, but we need to be home by milking time tonight."

Jenary looked out the window and tried not to be disappointed. Yet, she understood farm work. Jenary knew they needed the milk and eggs just like her family did. She leaned toward Sarah and whispered, "Even being together a little while is better than not getting to see you at all."

Sarah nodded, then drank her glass of milk. "I know."

Mother carried little Bobby into the kitchen. "Perhaps we can visit and make ice cream this summer."

After kissing the babies good-bye, Jenary hugged Sarah. "I'll see you before too long."

While Pa shook Uncle John's hand and spoke quietly to him, Mother hugged Aunt Elizabeth. "May God keep you under His wing of protection."

Jenary waved good-bye until the wagon disappeared over the hill. The red sand swirled into dust devils, then disappeared into the clear blue sky. She hurried back to the kitchen. "I'll wash the dishes."

Mother poured hot water into the dish pan. "After you rinse the dishes, just let them drip dry," she said. "I want to strip the beds. Your pa is building a fire so we can wash everything this morning."

After dipping the dishes in the hot water, Jenary laid them onto a clean towel to dry. She had just set the bent-up teakettle back on the stove when she heard the clop of horses' hooves in the yard.

She hurried to the front door. Mr. Masters leaned down. "Brought you a letter," he said. "Jenary, you're popular."

Billy ran around the house with Spot nipping at his heels. "I'm popular, too," he told the school teacher. "What does that mean?"

Mr. Masters leaned back and laughed. "I can see we need to get our school started, and soon!"

"Did you know that I fell into the creek?" Billy stated.

Mr. Masters hauled Billy up into the saddle in front of him. "Okay, Mr. Popular, you can tell me about it while we find your pa."

"He's around back building a fire under the wash pot," Billy said.

Jenary ran to the back room and ripped the envelope open. "Mother," she called out, "I got a letter. It's from Medicine Lodge. Oh the letter's from Susanne!"

Mother picked the sheets up and placed them in a bushel basket. "How wonderful! What does your friend say?"

Jenary read the letter, eagerly. "She misses me at school. The class is studying about the pioneer families pushing toward California.

"Susanne said that her Pa and Ma have been talking about moving to Oklahoma Territory. That is if they can find a claim."

Mother walked into the kitchen, gathered the dirty towels, and laid them into the basket. "That would be nice, if that's what Susanne's family decides."

"I want them to get a house close to us," Jenary said.

Mother pushed open the screen door. "Honey, you want Sarah to live closer. Now you want your friend to be our neighbor, too."

"If Susanne were here, she and I could make ice cream and bake sugar cookies," Jenary said. "It would be lots of fun."

Jenary stepped off the porch, hurried down the steps, then walked over to the wash pot. Jenary smiled when Mr. Masters looped the reins over a limb of the Elm tree, then lifted Billy off King. "Did you have a good ride?" she called out.

"Yeah! The horse bounces you up and down," her brother said, "but I like him!"

The school teacher walked over to Pa. "Need some help?"

Pa reached up from behind the iron pot and shook Mr. Master's hand. "We can always use help on wash day. It's a job keeping this fire hot."

The teacher shoved a big stick into the flame. "I guess I had better learn how to do this. Maggie's on her way to Oklahoma Territory."

Hearing Mr. Master's news, Jenary tagged along behind him while he gathered broken limbs. "When will Miss Reynolds get here?" she asked.

Mother stirred the clothes around with the cut-off broom handle. "We're anxious to meet your intended."

Mr. Masters laid the wood on the ground. "I'm expecting the families to arrive by the end of this week," he said. "Hopefully by Saturday so we can go into Elm Grove and meet the new minister."

Scurrying up to Mr. Master's side, Billy asked. "Can I go, too?"

Pa gripped Billy's shoulder. "Son, don't be impolite. You've been taught better. It's rude to go inviting yourself."

"It's all right," Mr. Masters said. "I'm not sure that my aunt and uncle can go into town on Saturday. If not, perhaps Billy and Jenary can accompany us. After all, Maggie and I may need a chaperone."

"Really?" Billy asked, excitedly. "What's a chaperone? Can I be one, Pa? Can I?"

"Let's wait until she arrives," Pa answered. "Then we'll see."

Jenary listened with wide open ears and a wild imagination while Mr. Masters described Miss Reynolds; What would she be like? How pretty would she be? Jenary expected Miss Reynolds to be as nice as Mr. Masters.

# Chapter Five
## Best Friends

Smoky flame from the kerosene lamp flickered. Jenary sat on the edge of the bed. She remembered her dear friend, Susanne. Outside, the distant yap of a coyote sounded. A whippoorwill called its melancholy song. 'This is a wild country' she thought, then turned back to her friend's letter. How Jenary missed her.

Jenary recalled playing the game of 'Jump The Rope' with Susanne and the other girls at school. Jenary smiled at the memory of how she and her friend had practiced and practiced the game of 'Jacks'.

Staring at the date on the envelope from Kansas, Jenary figured that Susanne must have mailed the letter just after the first of the year, January 1894. It sure took a long time for mail to arrive.

Jenary longed to send a letter back to Susanne. With the new post office in Elm Grove, she knew there was a way. Perhaps

Jenary could ask Mother to buy a stamp.

Last Saturday Pa and Mother went into town to trade eggs for coffee and sugar. Pa came home talking about the post office located on Main Street.

"The mail travels by stagecoach," Pa said, "kind of like the pony express that carried the mail from St. Louis, Missouri over the mountains to California."

After blowing out the light, Jenary lay down and pulled the sheet snugly to her chin. Mother and Pa worked hard to provide for their family. Jenary almost dreaded to ask favors from either one of them, but she wanted so badly to get a letter to Susanne.

Jenary's thoughts tumbled over and over. 'How serious is Susanne's pa about coming to Oklahoma Territory'? Jenary prayed that a claim would open up for Susanne and her family.

At breakfast, Jenary watched Pa's coffee cup. When he had drank the hot black liquid, and it went down below the half way mark, Jenary jumped to her feet and quickly refilled Pa's cup.

He sipped. "Thanks, Sis," he said. "I appreciate you being so polite and helping your mother, but what's going on? Do you want something special?"

Jenary leaned across the table. "Pa, do you remember my friend Susanne, back in Kansas?"

Pa leaned back in the chair. "Sort of. I'm trying to place her."

Breaking open a biscuit, Jenary placed a dab of fresh butter on the halves. "She lived down the road from us and came by every morning. We walked to school together. Pa, I need a stamp for that letter to Susanne."

"I heard that it costs two cents," Pa said, "but I reckon we could manage to get one."

"I remember Susanne," Mother said, pushing her plate away. "Didn't she have an older brother?"

"Matt!" Billy announced. "Sometimes he would let me ride on his shoulders when I was little. I'm too big for him to carry now!"

Jenary bit into her biscuit, trying to hide a threatening smile. Billy liked to brag. "Pa, in her letter, Susanne said that her parents were talking about coming out here."

Her pa hit his knee. "Of course! That would be Abe Strong and his missus," Pa said. "I talked and talked, trying to help our neighbors understand that this was probably our last chance for free land. I told them that we needed to band together when we made the run in that big race. Otherwise someone could steal our wagon and everything."

"Maybe they heard about the Cheyenne and Arapaho Indians," Mother said. "I heard in town that these tribes were moved from Kansas."

"Just like us!" Billy called out.

Mother patted his arm. "Not quite. We came because we wanted to."

Pa pushed away from the table. "It seems that the Cheyenne tribe didn't want to plant crops and learn to be farmers."

Jenary stacked the dishes in the dish pan. Surely Susanne's pa was not afraid of these Indians. After all there were Indians in Kansas. "Do you suppose there's a 160 acre claim for the Strongs?" Jenary asked.

"I'm not sure," Pa answered. "Some good and some not so good things have happened since we came down here. Look at John and Elizabeth's situation, but things have worked out for them. Who knows?"

Jenary would write a letter to Susanne. Maybe she would see her friend again. Pa had been talking about the Indians here in the Territory. Jenary missed her friend and she missed going to school. She wondered if she could borrow a book from Mr. Masters. Jenary and her family had left all of their friends and the life they knew back in Medicine Lodge. Perhaps she could learn more about the Indians and the Oklahoma Territory.

# Chapter Six
## Miss Reynold's Arrival

A cool afternoon breeze drifted lazily across the backyard. Jenary removed the dry clothes from the green bushes. She placed Pa and Billy's shirts and overalls in the basket. She carefully laid Mother's paisley printed dress and apron on top.

Mother had brought her wooden clothes pins, but Pa told them that it would be a while before he could put up a real clothes line.

Jenary knew that Pa felt bad. He wanted to put up the line now, but he needed to trade or barter for the wire. Then Pa would cut some poles from scrub Oak trees. Soon, Jenary and Mother could have a clothes line, just like the one back in Medicine Lodge.

Sighing Jenary's thoughts turned to her new dress and bonnet, hanging on a nail beside her bed. Last week, Mother had stayed up late sewing the pink polk-a dot dress and matching bonnet.

She felt proud of her new clothes. Her mother saved all the printed feed and flour sacks for school clothes, but Jenary knew that Mother had saved the eggs and milk and traded them for the pretty material at the Elm Grove Mercantile.

"You'll need a Sunday dress," Mother told her. "Several carpenters around town have almost finished the church house. I heard that a preacher and his family came to Elm Grove. They're staying with Jim and Cora Brown," she said. "We'll be having morning services next Sunday."

Jenary carried the basket to the house. She heard Pa, out in the field, calling the horses Prince and Sadie. Although dust filled the air, she saw Billy, just inside Pa's arms, standing behind the turning disc in the rich fertile ground.

"Ya, get up, Prince," Pa hollered. "Come on, Sadie."

Stepping onto the porch, Jenary called out, "Mother, come and see what Pa's doing! And Billy's helping."

"Pa's breaking up the ground to put in a garden," Mother said. "Billy pestered his pa until he let the boy get behind the horses too."

Leaning against the screen door, Jenary watched the horses pull the disc, leveling the dark red soil. "I remember our garden back in Medicine Lodge, but this garden looks bigger."

Mother patted Jenary's shoulder. "That's Pa," she said, in a teasing voice. "He always has such big plans for a garden. He'll want to start planting potatoes right away."

"Billy's old enough to hoe this year," Jenary stated. "He can help gather the green beans and potatoes."

Jenary turned at the sound of a clop-clop-clop. Her mother pushed the screen door open, then they stepped onto the porch. A horse with a buggy pulled into the yard.

"Look Mother," Jenary said, excitedly. "Mr. Masters has come and there's a lady with him."

"I figure that's his Miss Reynolds," Mother said.

"Yea," Jenary said. "I can't wait to meet her."

Ducking under the reins, Billy ran across the field and toward the buggy, with Spot racing after him. "Hi, Mr. Masters."

"Hi yourself," the school teacher said, ruffling Billy's hair. "Been helping your pa?"

"Yeah!" Billy exclaimed. "I got to hold the reins and everything!"

Mr. Masters laughed, then took the woman's hand and helped her out of the buggy. "I want you to meet Miss Maggie Reynolds."

Jenary's heart beat excitedly. She really liked the teacher's satin dress and the hat trimmed with a veil and highlighted by a white feather. It was sure different from the plain bonnets that Mother and Aunt Elizabeth wore.

Mother stepped forward. "Welcome to Oklahoma Territory!" she said. "When did you arrive?"

Miss Reynolds smiled. "We arrived at the families' homestead just before dark, day before yesterday."

"I bet you're still tired," Mother soothed. "Why don't you come inside? The coffee pot's on the stove or I can make tea."

Jenary watched as Mother offered a big welcome to Mr. Masters' soon-to-be missus. Jenary ran up the steps and opened the back screen door. She hoped she could be just like her mother someday.

"Are you going to be my teacher?" Billy asked.

Miss Reynolds laughed. "Possibly, but you're so tall that you may need to go into Mr. Masters' room."

Glancing at the teachers, Jenary said, "If both of you have your own classroom, that means that the new school house will be as big as the one back in Kansas."

Billy leaned lazily across the kitchen table. "So when are you getting married?" he asked, abruptly.

"Billy Joe, you stop asking such questions," Mother said. "Don't be impolite. Anyway, its none of your business."

Mr. Masters moved his chair closer to Billy. "Actually Miss Maggie and I hope that ours will be the first wedding in the new church house."

Mother filled glasses with tea and handed them to the teachers. "Jenary and I would be honored to bake your cake," Mother said. "That is if your aunt hasn't already offered."

"Let's see when the minister can marry us," Mr. Masters said, "then we'll make plans."

Mother wiped her hands on her apron. "It's almost dinner time," she said, looking over at the teachers. "You will stay and eat with us, won't you? Pa will be in shortly."

Miss Reynolds twisted in the chair. "We don't want to impose."

"I put on a big pot of soup this morning," Mother said. "I just need to make a pan of cornbread."

Jenary went to the cabinet and took down the soup bowls. She had helped Mother open the precious jars of preserved vegetables earlier that morning. She was thankful that her mother planned so well and could fix a good dinner, even for unexpected company.

"I hear Pa now," Mother said. She opened the oven door and peeked at cornbread turning a golden brown.

He washed at the bench, then stepped into the kitchen to

greet Miss Reynolds and Mr. Matthews. Minutes later, Mother set a pot of soup on the table, then took up the cornbread.

"So where are you going to live?" Pa asked.

Mr. Masters placed a dab of butter on a slice of hot bread. "Uncle Fred offered to give us a spot on the west side of his acreage," he said, "but I heard about a place or two just outside of Elm Grove. We plan to look into those."

"So we'll be fairly close to school," Miss Reynolds added.

Jenary wondered how she and Billy would get to school. They had walked across the pasture to town, back in Medicine Lodge, but there were ravines and gullies out here in Oklahoma Territory. She remembered how Pa had heard about the 'Sooners' hiding in the ravines. They waited to ambush the homesteaders and take their land.

Shuddering, Jenary felt glad there were not any 'Sooners' around now. "Mother told us that some of the town's people have plans for a school house," she said, sipping her tea.

"That's right," Mr. Masters agreed. "So many families are moving in and they want to get their children in school." He reached over and laid his hand over Maggie's. "We plan to be ready for them."

# Chapter Seven
## The Stampede

Early one Saturday morning, Jenary stirred a skillet of cream gravy while Mother peeked into the oven at a pan of golden brown biscuits. "We'll try to keep the bread warm until Pa and Billy finish milking the cows and feeding the herd."

Pa worked hard in the fields of wheat, but he was especially proud of the newly acquired cattle. Mother laughed when Pa became so excited, then she would pat his hand. Jenary knew she was proud too.

He had bartered with homesteaders who had left the territory. Now Pa had accumulated a fairly big herd. He knew every cow, where he had acquired her and all about her calves.

The back door slammed and Billy rushed into the kitchen. "Some of our cows are gone!"

Pa walked in and placed two buckets of milk on the counter. Mother poured two cups of coffee and handed one to Pa.

"Are they really gone?"

"It sure looks like it!" Pa said.

Jenary ran to the window. She heard a sound in the distance. "Is that thunder? Are we having another storm, Pa?"

Suddenly the ground shook and the house trembled. Pa jerked open the back door. "Look at all of those cattle! They're trampling everything in sight."

Mother stood next to Pa, wringing the corner of her apron. "They're coming awful close to the house!"

"And those cowboys are shouting, making the cows run faster," Billy said, in an excited voice. "Where did they come from?"

"They're probably from Texas!" Pa answered.

Billy picked up a stick of kindling. "I bet me and Spot can make them get off our land!"

Mother grabbed Billy's shirt tail. "Don't you dare go out there," she scolded. "The cattle will stomp you to death!"

"Mother's right son," Pa agreed. "Help me watch for the boss of the outfit. Maybe we can find out what's going on."

For what seemed like forever, Jenary felt the cows' hooves pound the ground. Through the red dust, she watched them trample Mother's lilac bush, then bend her wild red rose bush almost to the ground. "When are the cows going to stop coming? There's so many of them."

Pa stepped onto the porch, then pointed off in the distance. "Looks like the trail bosses coming our way."

Jenary watched three cowboys ride up to Pa and rein in their horses. "What do you mean driving your herd across our land?" Pa demanded.

A tall middle-age cowboy got off his horse and strode up

to Pa. "Sorry about that, folks. Our trail is further to the east, but a bunch of wild hogs frightened the cattle. We had a stampede on our hands. I'm mighty glad that we could turn the herd before they ran through your house."

"I'm sure grateful for that," Pa said, "but they've destroyed my east wheat field."

The trail boss whipped out a long dark leather billfold. "I want to pay you for any damages."

Pa scratched his head, then named a sum of money. "I appreciate your offer."

"And for Mother's rose and lilac bush," Billy added. "She's working hard planting them."

Pa laid a hand on Billy's shoulder. "It'll be all right, son."

"There's our cows," Billy called out, pointing to a bunch cattle near to the barn."

"Our cattle got too close to your herd," the trail boss said. "I'll have one of my cowboys cut your cows out and a couple more to boot for all of the trouble we've caused you."

Pa pushed his hat back on his head. "Thank you for the extra cows. I'm mighty glad to have them."

"It's our fault," the trail boss said, "and we want to make things right by you folks."

Jenary sat down on the steps. She watched the cowboys ride their horses up to the herd, then cut out Pa's five cows and three more.

"Did you see how their dog worked the herd?" Billy asked, running over to Jenary. "Maybe Spot can learn how to work like that."

Although she was pleased that Pa got their cows back along with the new ones, Mother's bushes were beat down to the ground

In one of Mr. Masters books, Jenary had read about the Cheyenne and Arapaho Indians. She also learned about these Texas trail drives.  It seemed that they knew about the lush buffalo grass that waved in the wind and shimmered in the hot sun.

However when the drivers used the trail to drive the herds to market in Dodge City, they flattened the Cherokees' lands. Jenary was glad to know more of these tribes of Indians and about the Texas trail drivers. Yet she hoped that there would never be another cattle drive across her family's land.

A late orange afternoon sun drooped lower while a half-moon, rising in the east, hid behind high clouds. Mother put the kettle on the stove and Jenary stacked the dishes from supper in the dish pan.

In the distance crickets tuned up for their nightly serenade. Pa sat the table while Mother reached for the coffee pot on the back burner. She looked over at Pa. "Want more coffee?"

"Yes," he replied. "I brought the sack of potatoes we saved back from last year's crop," Pa said. He looked over at Billy. "Sprout and I turned and harrowed the ground for the garden spot. We need to cut the eyes of the spuds so we can get them ready to plant."

While the dishes soaked in the hot soapy water, Jenary sat on the back steps helping Pa and Mother. She reached into the gunny sack and grabbed a handful of potatoes. "How many do we need to cut?" she asked.

Pa cut one and laid it into a galvanized pan. "Sis we need to plant enough for this spring and to keep us through the winter."

"These potatoes will taste good when the snow is on the ground," Mother assured Jenary. "Best pull out more potatoes."

Jenary watched Pa and Mother each cut a potato into big

hunks.  It seemed like she had sat on the step since forever. She remembered planting time back in Kansas.

However Pa was not able to dig as many potatoes as he had planted. Jenary heard him tell Mother that they did not get the yield, because the ground was worn out. She hoped this rich soil would give their family many baskets of firm potatoes.

"Why do you cut them into such big pieces?" Jenary asked. "Couldn't we fry the left over part?"

Mother pulled the paring knife through another potato. "If we don't leave a big piece around the eye, the new potato won't have enough to live on until it leafs out."

"Oh," Jenary said, "I see."

She gazed across the back yard watching Billy walking toward the house, arms filled with small limbs. "This is the third load, Pa," Billy boasted. "Do you think it's enough?"

"Be sure the wood box behind the stove is full," Pa told him. "We'll need some kindling brought in too."

Billy stacked the limbs next to the porch. "I filled Mother's box first, then brought in the kindling."

"Good boy," Pa said. He reached over and squeezed his shoulder. "I appreciate your help. Now you best check to see you've put out hay for Prince, Sadie, and Nellie."

Billy shuffled from one foot to the other while Spot nipped at his heels. "I already filled their stalls."

"Thanks again son," Pa said, with affection in his voice.

Jenary's heart swelled to almost overflowing. She knew that deep in Pa's heart he loved her and Billy just like Mother did. Yet he had not always hugged them. After Aunt Elizabeth and Uncle John's baby died, things had changed. Pa made sure to give Jenary and Billy a hug every night, before bedtime.

The next morning, Mother stacked the breakfast dishes beside the pan of hot water. "I hope it won't take too long to get the potatoes planted," she said. "It's Saturday and we need to polish our shoes and take a bath tonight. Tomorrow is the first church service in the new church."

Pa gazed out the kitchen window. "We finish when we finish."

Mother wanted all of them to attend the first church services. She hoped to meet all of the families that had settled around Elm Grove. To Pa nothing was more important than the crops. Jenary looked at Mother. "We'll work as fast as we can," she promised.

With Pa carrying a bucket of water, Jenary and Billy went to the far end of the garden. Jenary dug a five inch hole, then Pa placed a piece of potato in, with the eye turned up.

Jenary raked dirt over the seed potatoes, and Billy poured a dipper full on water on each hill. "Pa," he called, "are we going to have some baby chickens this year?"

Their Pa started on another row. "Our four hens will be setting before long. Maybe some little chicks will hatch from those eggs."

"And we can watch the babies peck out of the shell," Billy said, excitedly.

Pa laughed. "But we don't touch the little chicks when they are pecking out of the shell, do we son?"

Billy raked the dirt into the hole and pounded it down. He shook his head. "No sir, we don't."

From under her bonnet, Jenary glanced up at Billy. Last year her brother had been determined to help the chicken crack the egg shell. Luckily Mother saw Billy just in time. She explained that we could not touch those eggs. Not even if the chickens were almost out of the shell.

After the hoe and bucket were placed back in the barn, Jenary, with Billy scampering after her, hurried up the back steps and pulled open the screen door. "We got all of the potatoes planted," Jenary told Mother. "I want to wash up and go to bed."

Standing beside the cook stove, Mother poured more hot water into the wash tub. "I've got this ready for you to take a bath."

Jenary flopped down in a chair. "I'm too tired to take one tonight."

"Nonsense," Mother chided. She handed Jenary a bar of lye soap. "I've saved this special. Just for you. Come and get in, honey. I'll keep everyone out until you're finished."

Quickly Jenary undressed and stepped into the water. She scrubbed off the garden dirt, then rubbed the suds through her hair. "This warm water feels good."

Mother dipped a pitcher in the tub and poured water through Jenary's hair to rinse out the suds, then handed her a towel. "I want all the family to go to church in the morning."

Jenary quickly dried herself and slipped into her gown. "We've waited so long for the new church," she told Mother. "I hope Pa goes with us."

"He will now," Mother said. "The potatoes are in the ground. Now go on to bed. It's Billy's turn to get cleaned up."

Lying in the dark, Jenary thought about the letter she wanted to write to Susanne. She planned to tell her friend about Elm Grove. She wanted her to know that the teachers had arrived and the church house was finished and ready for the first Sunday service. Now the men were building a school.

Jenary heard Billy complain, then water splashed. She listened to Mother scolding her brother. Jenary smiled. She would tell Susanne about Billy and his trouble with water.

First he jumped into Persimmon Creek after Spot. Now the bath water was probably all over the kitchen floor. Then a tornado came and a stampeding herd of Texas cattle. Jenary hoped with all of her heart that Susanne and her family could come to the Oklahoma Territory. She needed a close friend.

# Chapter Eight
## Bobcats and Wedding Plans

A warm breeze danced through the clearing. Green buds were clustered on the branches of the Elm trees. The fragrance of wild honeysuckle drifted in through the open window. It seemed to Jenary that the Oklahoma Territory was a good place to live.

After dinner Jenary helped Mother clear the table. "Why don't you and Billy walk over to the blackberry patch and each of you pick a bucket full of berries. I want to make a cobbler."

Pa drank his tea, then looked up, his eyes twinkled. "Uhm, Blackberry."

Jenary smiled. No one could make a cobbler like Mother. "All right, but where's Billy?"

Pushing away from the table, Pa laughed. "He and Spot are bringing in the wood. We don't want to run short during all this cooking for the wedding."

Taking two buckets off the shelf, Jenary pushed open the

door. "Here he comes now."

Billy dusted off his hands. "That's all the wood they'll need for a while."

Holding out the buckets, Jenary said. "Let's get some blackberries."

"Now?" Billy asked. "Spot and I worked. Now we want to play."

"C'mon," she said, "let's go."

Pa stepped out onto the back porch. "You better leave Spot at home or you'll never get any berries picked."

Through the trees and west of the house, stood a clearing. The bushes were loaded with plump juicy berries. Jenary handed Billy a bucket.

"Ow," he grumbled, "these thorns hurt."

She set her half filled bucket on the ground. "I'll help you fill yours up," she offered. "We'll finish quicker."

"Yea! Thanks, Sis."

The sharp briars stuck, but Jenary gently pulled the berries off the bush.

"Look," Billy called out. "My bucket is full."

"Come and help me fill mine," Jenary said.

"All right," he replied. Billy pulled at the bush. "Oh!"

"It won't be long now," she soothed, then hurriedly tossed berries into her bucket. "I think we have enough for Mother's cobbler. Let's get yours and go . . . ."

Jenary screamed.

Billy rushed over. "It's a kitten. No. It's two little kittens."

Jenary stared at the honey-colored cats. "They're little Bobcats. They like your berries. Look at the stains on their paws."

"The 'kitties' want to play," Billy said, laughing.

"You can't play with them," she scolded.

"Grrr!" They heard a loud growl. The bushes shook and a huge honey-colored head appeared.

"It's a Bobcat," her brother whispered in fright. "A big Bobcat!"

"That's their mama," Jenary replied. She tried to ignore the fear gripping her heart. She had to protect her little brother. After all he was her only brother. "Let's go, but don't run."

"What if the Bobcat follows?" Billy asked. "She can jump a long ways."

"If we leave her babies alone, the mama cat will leave us alone." At least Jenary hoped this was true. She realized she could not allow her brother to see any fear, but Jenary could not wait to get home.

Quickly, she hurried through the grove of Elm and scrub Oak trees, then looked back. She did not see the Bobcat. She hoped the mama had taken her babies and left.

When she first saw their house, Jenary thought she had never before been so glad to be home.

Billy dashed up to her side. "Let's tell Pa and Mother!"

"We're home," Jenary called out, when she and her brother hurried into the kitchen.

"We saw little Bobcats and their mama chased us away!" Billy shouted.

Pa frowned, then turned. "Meredith, get my gun!"

Jenary reached for her mother's hand. "She didn't follow us through the woods."

Her brother smiled. "The little kittens turned over our bucket of blackberries."

Chuckling Pa said, "I bet you wanted to play with the little cats."

Although Jenary felt bad about not getting the blackberries for Mother's cobbler, she was thankful to be safe at home.

The sun tried to peek out from among the clouds on Sunday morning. Jenary thought this would be the day to meet the other families of Elm Grove. She hoped that they all attended this first church service.

Mother hurried over to Jenary. "Let me button your dress," she said. "I found a ribbon and tacked it onto your bonnet."

While Mother fastened the Sunday dress, Jenary touched the pink ribbon. "Thank you, Mother. Thanks for sewing this outfit for me."

"It turned out pretty," Mother said. She gazed at Jenary. "Pretty, just like you. Let me brush the tangles out of your hair."

Jenary gritted her teeth, then closed her eyes and tried not to think of every pull of the brush. Finally Mother placed the bonnet firmly on Jenary's head and tied the ribbon in a bow under her chin.

"Where's Billy?" Mother asked. "It's time to leave."

Jenary realized that her mother wanted everything to be just right this morning. Jenary hurried to the front door. "They're all ready in the wagon. They're waiting for us."

Pa had swept the wagon out, wiped off the front seat and placed a folded quilt in the back end of the wagon for Jenary and Billy. "Giddyup," Pa called out to Prince and Sadie. "Giddyup!"

"Woof!"

Jenary looked back toward the house. Spot ran lickety split behind the wagon.

"Go back!" Billy scolded. "Go back!"

Jenary sighed when the little dog stopped, panting with a tongue hanging out. He looked so sad. She glanced over at Billy. He watched Spot until the wagon climbed a hill.

Prince and Sadie trotted down the road and quickly covered the two and one-half miles into town. Jenary could not believe how much Elm Grove had changed since she and her family first arrived in Oklahoma Territory.

Jenary gazed at Elm Grove's Main Street. Mother had been right. Almost all of the tents, that had been used by the homesteaders, had been replaced by wooden buildings made with lumber hauled in by heavy wagons from eastern Indian Territory.

She raised herself onto her knees. Where was the school house? She heard a bell ring, but it did not chime like the bell on their church back in Kansas.

When Pa turned the corner, Jenary saw a crowd of people standing in front of a white washed building. Some were talking, while others began walking up the steps.

Inside, wooden benches lined both sides of the church house from front to back. Up front a stand held a Bible and a hymnal. Mother walked up the aisle, stopped three rows back, then scooted across the bench. Pa took off his hat and followed. Billy scampered behind them, then flopped down on the seat beside Pa.

Jenary walked slowly, glancing around the room at all of the people crowded into the pews. She had heard Pa and Uncle John talk about the banks that were closing back east.

Fred Masters told Pa that people were losing their jobs back in Illinois. Many of those families had arrived in Oklahoma Territory. Just like Jenary's family, they came to make a new start in life.

A man stood in front of the pulpit and introduced himself as the song leader. He opened a song book and began singing the hymn, "Count Your Blessings."

Although there was no piano or organ or other hymnals, the congregation's voices blended beautifully, "Name Them One By One," the leader's deep voice sang. "Count Your Many Blessings, See What God Has Done."

The new minister, with red hair and bushy eye brows, stepped beside the song leader. "My family and I came from Nebraska to be with you good folks," he announced. "I'm Reverend Aaron Cooper."

He pointed toward the front row where a dark haired woman held a baby boy with red hair. Two little girls nestled beside their mother. "I would like for you to meet my wife, Peggy, my little son, Adam and my daughters, Kathleen and Melanie."

At the close of the service, Reverend Cooper said, "We are thankful for everyone who came and joined us this Sunday morning."

Then the minister glanced at Mr. Masters. "We want to invite you to come to our first wedding in the Elm Grove Community Church. Our school teachers, Mr. Masters and Miss Reynolds are to be married two weeks from today. They want all of you to come and spend the day with them!

"We'll have a 'Getting Acquainted', dinner on the grounds after church. The couple's ceremony will be at 2:00 P.M. Now let's all stand for the benediction."

Thoughts of Mr. Masters and Miss Maggie's wedding fluttered around in Jenary's mind. She had heard Mother talk about people getting married, but Jenary had never been to a wedding. She could do a lot of things to help.

After dinner Mother sat on the porch, mending the hole in the knee of Billy's overalls while Pa worked down at the barn. Jenary found a piece of white paper, picked up a pencil, then sat down at the kitchen table. Jenary gazed out the window.

Dear Susanne,

I really miss you. I wish we could play 'Jacks' together again. I still have the handkerchief that you embroidered for me.

I sure hope that you and your folks can come to live here in the Oklahoma Territory. Remember how we used to walk to school together?

Our teacher, Mr. Masters, has arrived and now his missus-to-be, Miss Reynolds has come. We'll have a big dinner and a wedding for Mr. Masters and Miss Reynolds.

I wish you were here. We would have so much fun helping plan the wedding.

Maybe your pa can find a place real close to our land. Hurry and write to me.

Your best friend,
Jenary.

She folded the letter and slipped it into the envelope. She would tell Susanne the funny stories about Billy when she and her family arrived in the Oklahoma Territory.

Bright and early the following morning, Pa answered a knock at the back door. "Got any coffee?" Fred Masters asked.

"Sure," Pa said. "You folks come on in and sit a spell. A fresh pot is on the stove."

"The missus dragged me out of bed before daylight," Fred grumbled. "She insisted that we needed to get an early start on the wedding plans so we can get Blake and Maggie hitched."

Standing beside Mother, Jenary saw her wink at Missus Masters. Jenary had liked the school teacher from the very start. Now she realized how much she was beginning to like Mr. Masters' uncle and aunt.

"There's lots to do," Missus Masters said. "We need to figure out how many cakes and pies to bake other than the special cake itself."

"We want everyone who comes to the dinner to have enough to eat," Mother agreed.

"With the wedding cake and all," Aunt Belle Masters said, "we best get started getting all the food ready a few days before the big day."

Jenary could not wait for Mother and Missus Masters to begin cooking for the church dinner and special ceremony. Jenary hope they would need her help, especially with making the wedding cake. What excitement! It was going to be a beautiful wedding, the first in Elm Grove, Oklahoma Territory.

# Chapter Nine
## The Wedding

When the special Sunday arrived, a warm breeze floated around the church building. Lilac bushes had been planted and now sweet smells of Spring drifted through the air.

A week before the first wedding in the Elm Grove Community church, Aunt Belle gathered ingredients for the wedding cake. Mother planned to bake smaller cakes to be served after the ceremony. Smells of cinnamon wafted through the air and lingered in the kitchen.

Jenary had stayed up last night helping Mother fix the potatoes, eggs and sweet pickles for the potato salad. She had added bacon grease to the green beans, then stirred the filling for Mother's cherry pies.

Since Miss Reynolds' parents could not come to the ceremony, she had carefully packed her mother's wedding dress and brought it all the way to the Oklahoma Territory. In this special dress, Miss Reynolds would look radiant.

"Everything is ready for the wedding, today " Mother said, when Will and Uncle Fred began unloading the wagon.

"Let's take the wedding cake into the church house, "Aunt Belle said, "we'll leave it on a table at the back."

"Someone will need to watch it," Mother told her. "Otherwise one of the children will take a hunk of it during the service."

Jenary turned away to hide a smile. She really hoped they were not referring to Billy. However she knew he had watched Mother and Missus Masters put the white frosting on the three layer cake.

"The people from church can give them a pounding," Mother said. "Since Blake and Miss Maggie will be the school teachers, we'll invite all Elm Grove."

Jenary listened and tried to remember other times she had heard about a 'pounding'. Back in Medicine Lodge, all the women sewed sheets, pillow cases and cup towels for the newly married folks. The people also gave them a pound of coffee, sugar, flour, and cans of fruits and vegetables. This was a way of helping newly wed folks begin their lives.

During the church services, Reverend Cooper stood behind the pulpit and preached about God's love. "We live by faith," he told the congregation.

The song leader sat on the front bench. Following the sermon, with his deep voice, he lead the congregation in singing the closing song, "God Be With You 'till We Meet Again."

Jenary stood on the last step of the church house. She gazed at the long table, laden with food. A wave of surprise swept over her. Somehow they had set up a table and everyone had brought food. She figured all the church ladies, like her mother, had cooked all through Saturday night.

Mother touched Jenary's arm. "Honey, go fill your plate while everyone is visiting and getting acquainted. That's what our school teachers want the town folks to do."

Walking down the hill, Jenary looked over at crowd, gathered under the big Elm tree. "Look Mother," she said. "There's Mr. Masters and Miss Reynolds!"

"Everyone's stopped to visit. Let's get our food," Mother urged. "then we'll walk over and say hello."

Jenary walked beside her mother as she introduced herself to the new women who had come to the dinner. "This my daughter," Mother said. "And the wild boy running around is my son, Billy."

Lingering a moment, Jenary thought. 'Mother is beginning to get acquainted with everyone'. How she wanted to learn about making friends, just like her mother.

The women had cooked fried chicken, baked golden brown biscuits, fixed potato salad, and cooked homegrown green beans. Jenary's heart overflowed with gladness at the lighthearted laughter.

Later, Jenary watched the mothers place the food back into the wooden boxes, then clean up the dirty dishes. The wedding would soon happen.

Billy ran up to Jenary. "Come on," he called out, excitely. "Mr. Masters and the preacher are already in the churh house!"

"Let's hurry," Jenary said. "We want to see Miss Reynolds come in."

Mother walked up and firmly took Billy's hand. "Uncle Fred is going to walk the bride down the aisle. Let's go, Pa is waiting for us."

Tiny pearls sparkled around the collar on the white satin dress and the edge of the sleeves. Jenary thought she had never seen anything so beautiful. She gazed at Miss Reynolds who smiled as she stepped up beside Mr. Masters. Mother sniffed, then blinked tears. "It's all so pretty."

The school teachers said their vows and were pronounced husband and wife.

Later they stood behind the table at the back of the church house. The wedding cake had been placed at the end of the table beside a big milk-glass bowl.

Jenary could not wait to taste the pretty cake and drink some of the punch. She looked at the smiles on the newly wed's faces. With the missus' help, Jenary knew that Mr. Masters would likely be able to visit all the families that moved into the Oklahoma Territory.

Suddenly, a small rodent with a bushy tail ran in the side door, across the room and under the table. Then he scampered up the aisle between the benches.

"It's a squirrel!" shouted Aunt Belle. "Someone do something!"

"Woof! Woof!"

"That sounds like Spot," Mother said, "but he couldn't have come all the way into town."

Before Jenary could find the words to speak, Spot chased the squirrel. While the rodent dashed around people's feet, the dog knocked over chairs. Everyone attempted to stand back while Billy chased Spot. Jenary leaned against the wall, trying desperately not to laugh.

Mother hurried after her son and his dog. "Stop this," she called after Billy. "You're spoiling their wedding!"

Pa opened the front door. "What's going on?"

Spot nipped at the squirrel's tail as the trail of desperados dashed out the door.

"Come back, Spot," Billy called out, running lickety split his the dog.

To Jenary's amazement, Mr. Masters chuckled. "I suspect this has been the liveliest wedding so far around these parts," he said.

That night, Mother and Pa sat at the supper table, eating cornbread and milk. "Did you ever see the like?" Pa asked.

"I couldn't believe my eyes," Mother said.

Billy sipped his milk. "Can you believe that Spot followed us all the way to town? At least Mr. Masters was not mad."

Jenary felt thankful that the school teachers seemed to enjoy Billy and Spot's adventure along with the cake and punch.

That night, Jenary got out her letter to Susanne. "P.S," she wrote. "You should have been here to see what happened at the wedding."

Quickly, Jenary told her friend about the afternoon. Then added. "I can't wait to see you. We can walk to school together, just like we used to."

Earlier, Mother had told Jenary about the men in town and how they worked late every night. They tried to finish the school house before they needed to put in their crops. Jenary knew she would be busy helping Mother in the garden.

By the time school started, she hoped that Mr. Masters and his missus' school rooms would be filled. She was grateful that she and her family had decided to come to the Oklahoma Territory.

Jenary liked the new church building and the minister. She had noticed him attempting to squash his laughter, when the two desperadoes got loose, but he was unsuccessful. Even Mr. Master found humor in the episode. With these teachers, Jenary knew school would be fun, like it had been in Kansas.

## Part III
## Chapter One
Oklahoma Territory-1894
School Days

A hot August sun beat down on the grassy plains. Mirages of heat waves shimmered across the drought-stricken land. A slight breeze blew dust devils in the sand across the school yard. Twelve-year-old Jenary Kay Evans was excited. This was the first day of school in Elm Grove.

One Sunday last spring, after church and pot-luck dinner on the ground, the town's people began building the school house. It was constructed of left-over planks from the merchants' and families' homes. In addition, the carpenters had used the logs that the people had gathered.

The school had a big room, with a long coat rack at the back. They planned to add a smaller room for the younger children someday.

The Johnson family had brought two old desks from back home and donated them, when they settled in the Oklahoma Territory. Mr. Tom Green and Jim Brown, who had school aged children, swapped out labor with one of the carpenters to build more desks.

Jenary was thrilled to watch the school house nearing completion. Each Sunday she looked over the congregation, trying to count the school-age children. Mr. Masters and his missus gradually visited in all of the houses around Elm Grove to welcome the students-to-be.

Pa took the small bell, that had called them to church all summer, and hung it beside the front door of the school. The congregation hoped they would soon be able to obtain a big bell for the church building.

When Jenary arrived on Monday morning, she was thrilled to see the new white washed school house. She did not know how the carpenters managed, but they had completed the school house. Above the door, hung the sign, 'Rockford School'. Smiling, Jenary hurried up the steps and opened the heavy Oak door. Twelve school desks sat on the waxed plank floor.

Jenary walked to the front of the room where Mr. Masters sat behind an old scarred teacher's desk. Fastened on the wall behind him was a slate blackboard.

They even carried Miss Maggie's piano inside. It occupied the far side of the room. Jenary glanced at the sheen on the wood of the piano, and wondered who gave the musical instrument to the school. Everything looked beautiful to her.

"Let's stand and salute the flag," Mr. Masters said. "I pledge allegiance to the flag . . . ."

"And we'll recite the Lord's Prayer together," he told the

class. "Our Father who Art in Heaven . . . ."

Miss Maggie sat down at the piano. "Let's all sing a hymn that we learned at church last Sunday morning. "Bringing In The Sheaves."

Voices began to build, filling the hollow room. "We shall come rejoicing, bringing in the sheaves . . . ."

"Now," Mr. Masters said, "each of you can stand and introduce yourself. Tell the class where you lived before you came here. Let's start on the front row."

A tall girl, with dark red hair, stood up. "I'm Kelsianne." She pointed to the little black haired girl sitting beside her. "This is my little sister, Jessee. We're all the way from Nebraska."

"I'm Frances," the next girl, on the row said. "We came from Missouri."

The girl in the row behind Kelsianne stood. "I'm Adelaide," she said, "from Arkansas."

"Now we have the twins," Mr. Master said, smiling. "You boys stand and tell us your names."

"I'm Jared."

"And I'm Jacob, but you can call me Jake."

"It's difficult to tell them apart," Miss Maggie said.

"We came from Colorado," Jared said. "Our cousin, Justin is from Texas."

"Is he coming to school?" Mr. Masters asked.

"He's helping his pa," Jake said, "but his ma sure wants him to come and learn."

Billy jumped to his feet. "My sis and I are from Medicine Lodge, Kansas. We brought Spot with us. He's a big help."

Jenary stood. 'Yes, Spot was a lot of help. He had helped Billy fall in the creek.' "My brother's right. We're from Kansas. We came in the Cherokee Outlet Land Rush."

How glad Jenary was to have four girls in school. She felt hopeful that they would all become friends. During noon recess, she talked to her new friends.

"Maybe Mr. Masters will let us play 'Hide And Go Seek,' at lunch time tomorrow."

"We could play, 'Jump The Rope'," Frances said.

Jessee inched closer to Kelsianne. "I want to play, too."

Red dust devils spiraled across the school yard. Jenary wiped her face with her handkerchief. "We don't have a rope, but maybe Pa has one that we can use," she said. "I'll bring it to school in the morning."

She glanced at Adelaide. "Do you want to play with us?"

The girl from Arkansas nodded. "Yes, but I want to bring something else to school."

"What's that?" Kelsianne asked.

Jenary leaned closer to a new friend. "Tell us what you want to bring to school."

"My guitar," she said.

Frances clasped her hands together. "Do you play the guitar?"

"Yes. My uncles taught me," Adelaide said.

When school was dismissed, Jenary called to her brother, "Let's go Billy.''Pa need help milking the cows."

"I bet I can beat you home," he called out, scampering down the steps. He ran across the school yard. "Hurry."

"Wait up," she called out. "I'm coming. Don't run off and leave me."

That morning, walking across the pasture in the cool air, the path did not seem so long. Yet, in the late afternoon the grassland seemed to stretch on and on. Finally, in the distance, Jenary saw the frame house Pa had built for the family.

She looked out across the field and a warm smile brightened her face. Her pa was always busy doing farm work and the everyday chores. Farming never let even the weary pause for long. He would soon put away the plow and go milk the cows. Before dark, Pa would feed the herd of cattle. "We're home," she called out to Mother.

Billy skipped up, with Spot trailing close behind. "I beat you," he boasted to Jenary. Nibbling on a warm cookie he sneaked from the plate, he smiled.

Mother pointed her finger at Billy. "Now don't go spoil your supper, young man," she scolded. "Go help Pa get the chores finished. It's almost time to eat."

Jenary stopped beside mother. "What do you need me to do to help get supper ready?"

Mother slipped her arm around Jenary. "Most of the supper is cooking. Let's get the cornbread ready."

When they all sat down to eat, Jenary looked over at Pa. "Can I take a piece of rope to school in the morning?"

"Whatever for?" her pa asked.

"My friends and I want to play 'Jump The Rope' at recess."

"You can take the piece I use to tie Nell. She'll be in the pasture all day."

Jenary popped up from her chair and hugged Pa. "Thank you so much! I promise I'll bring it back after school."

Billy bit into a potato. I'm going to take my marbles in the morning," he announced. "Jake and Jared came to school yesterday. We're going to play together."

Mother reached for a bowl. "Are those the Johnson boys?"

"Yeah," Billy said. "They're twins. I wish I had a twin."

Mother looked toward Heaven and gave a deep sigh of relief

"Thank you God for giving us only one of Billy."

Billy ate a bite of bread and spoke at the same time. "Jared said that his cousin, Justin might come to school soon."

"Mr. Masters talked about all the things we're going to study this Fall," Jenary said. "Jake and Jared like to talk in class, especially Jake."

"Tattle tale," Billy said. "You're a tattle tale."

Pa shook a stern finger at Billy. "Don't you boys be giving your teacher any trouble."

"We won't," Billy assured him. "I'm just glad to have some boys in school to play with. I'm getting tired of girls," he said, casting a teasing stare at Jenary.

After she helped Mother with the dishes, Jenary put on her night gown and slipped into bed. She glanced across the room at Billy. "Are you awake?"

"No!"

"If you're asleep, how can you talk?"

"I talk in my sleep," Billy said, then snored loudly.

Smiling at his humor, Jenary laughed. She felt sleepy and closed her eyes. She could hardly wait to go to school tomorrow. Mr. Masters promised they would began studying about the Indians and how they came to this Territory.

# Chapter Two
## The Abandoned Cabin

Mr. Masters wrote the arithmetic problems on the board when a knock sounded at the front door. He pointed at six-foot Justin. "See who's there."

Justin slid from his desk, he sauntered to the door. When he opened the door, Mr. Strong, his missus and two children stood on the porch.

The family stepped into the room. Astonished, Jenary put both hands over her mouth. She had written to her best friend, hoping that Susanne and her family would somehow come to the Oklahoma Territory. Yet, she could not believe that her friend had arrived.

"We want to start our youngun's." the pa said. He turned to the children. "This is Matt and Susanne."

Mr. Masters hurried across the room and extended his hand to Mr. Strong. "Welcome! Come in. Children please find a seat at a desk," he suggested.

When Susanne and Matt settled in, the teacher looked toward the class. "I want everyone to introduce yourself to our new students. Please stand and say your name."

After everyone introduced themselves to Matt and Susanne, Jenary stood. "They know my brother Billy and me," she said. "We all went to school together back in Medicine Lodge."

Jenary was excited! She was glad that Susanne had chosen to sit in the seat across from her. She wanted to ask her friend a dozen questions. "Did your ma and pa find a claim?" she whispered. "Do you have a soddy to live in?" Holding her breath, Jenary waited for Susanne to answer.

Her eyes darted anxiously around the room. "We live in town right now," Susanne whispered, in reply.

Mr. Masters silently approached. "Do you girls think you could possibly wait until lunch and recess to visit?"

Bright red heat of embarrassment crept up Jenary's neck. She could not look at Mr. Masters. She had never been called down by a teacher, especially Mr. Masters, a family friend. Did he not understand that she had not seen Susanne in over a year?

When the noon bell rang, Jenary grabbed her bucket, then dashed outside with her special friend. "I'm so glad you're here. Let's go sit under the trees."

Susanne picked up her syrup bucket. "All right," she replied, as giddy as her friend.

Jenary pulled a sausage biscuit out of her bucket. "Now, tell me all about your trip down here," Jenary said. "Where are you staying?"

"Pa and Ma have pitched a tent over by Smitty's Black Smith shop," Susanne told her. "Mr. Smith told Pa that he has plenty of room and would welcome the company."

Jenary nibbled on a biscuit, then glanced at Susanne. "Well I'm just glad you're here."

"Pa hopes we can stay," Susanne said. "He told Ma that he wants to homestead, but hasn't found an empty claim, yet."

"We'll ask my pa," Jenary told her friend, proudly. "He knows all the 'goings on' in the territory."

Billy and Matt ran across the school yard and slid to a stop. Leaning his tall frame against a tree, Matt said, "Billy told me about a claim on the other side of Persimmon Creek."I decided that we want to go exploring after school."

"Yeah," Billy confirmed. "Where Uncle John and Aunt Elizabeth were going to live."

"Pa explained about claim-jumpers taking that land," Jenary said. She glanced at Susanne. "The soldiers from Camp Supply tried to keep those 'Sooners' from settling on a homestead."

"Did the soldiers really come?" Susanne asked.

"They may have driven those bad men off Uncle John's land," Billy said. "Let's go after school. We'll see if they're really gone."

Later in class, Jenary's thoughts raced. She could hardly keep her mind on the arithmetic problems that Mr. Masters was writing on the board. What if the soldiers made those men get off that 160 acres? Maybe Susanne and Matt could live there. 'There's not too much water in the creek now.' she thought.

"Write down each problem," the teacher told the class. Work on them at home and in the morning I'll take up your homework to grade."

Although Jenary liked learning, she could hardly wait for the school bell to ring. Perhaps she and Susanne could tag along with

Matt and Billy and explore the old claim. "We'd better ask Mother and Pa," Jenary explained, before committing to the exploration.

"We'd better go ask our ma too," Matt said. "She'll worry if we don't come on home from school, especially our first day."

Susanne reached for Jenary's hand. "Maybe you and Billy can come by the blacksmith shop."

"Can we go over to Billy and Jenary's house?" Matt asked his mother, when they reached the blacksmith shop. "Ma, it's a long time since we've seen them."

"I know you've missed your friends," she told him. "You and Susanne can go for a while, but you need to be home before dark."

Before the words left Mrs. Strong's mouth, the children scampered away. "Come on," Matt said. "Let's go exploring!"

When Jenary, Billy and their friends hurried across the pasture toward their white washed frame house, Spot ran to meet them before they reached the yard. The little dog ran and jumped up on Billy's leg.

"Hi boy," Billy said, stroking the little brown and white ball of fur. "Meet my friend, Matt and his sister."

Matt reached down and patted Spot's head. "He's a good little friend."

"Yes he is," Billy assured him.

Jenary hurried up the steps and pushed open the door. "Mother, look who's come," she announced, excitedly.

Billy rushed in front of Jenary. "And we want to go exploring!"

Hurrying across the room to Susanne and Matt, Mother said, "Come in the house. Susanne, your blond curls have grown past your shoulders. Look at you, Matt, you're almost as tall as your pa."Now, tell me what news did you bring us from Medicine Lodge?"

Matt pushed a lock of sandy-colored hair away from his face, then leaned quietly  against the door jamb. "Everything's about the same as when you left," he replied. "Not much excitement, not like here."

Smiling, Jenary reached for her mother's hand. "We want Susanne and Matt to see Persimmon Creek," she said, smiling. "I want to show them the place where Billy fell in."

"That was after the tornado," Mother explained, nodding. "But what about your chores?"

"We'll do everything when we get back!" Billy said, in a pleading voice.

Susanne twisted a stand of blond hair around her finger. "Matt and I will stay and help, we promise."

"All right," Mother relemted, "but don't be gone too long. You'll need to get things done up around here and Susanne and Matt must go home before dark."

Billy ran toward the kitchen door. "We will," he called over his shoulder. "Come on. I'll show you the creek."

With her brother, Matt, Spot and Susanne running behind her, Jenary led the way toward Persimmon Creek. Although many of the bright flowers had wilted, small vines covered with dark green leaves twined around the large wild grape vines.

Billy stopped at edge of the creek. "That's where Spot jumped in!"

"And my brother followed his dog into the water!" Jenary explained.

Matt stepped close. "Can we see the claim from here?"

"Not yet. It's just up the creek from the place where Sis pulled me out! Billy called out. "C'mon, I'll show you!"

Matt tagged behind Billy and the boys jumped over the underbrush that had grown along the bank of the creek. Jenary and Susanne watched in horror when Billy's feet became tangled in small vines.

Jenary breathed a sigh of relief when he pulled loose and hurried on. "Be careful," she called out.

Sliding to a stop, Billy pointed across Persimmon Creek. "That's the place right there."

Matt leaned closer. "Doesn't look like anyone's there."

Jenary watched for a moment, before standing on her tiptoes and attempting to peek in the window of the soddy. It was a dugout, sitting back under a hill with a frame building in front. "Those claim jumpers must have left. This place is empty."

"Maybe Ma and Pa can get this place," Matt said. "It would sure beat living in a tent."

Susanne walked to the edge of the edge of the water. "With only the front part of the soddy setting out, we can't see inside. I wish we could get a better look."

Billy stood at the edge of the creek. "It's not very deep. I bet we can just step across!"

Matt sat on the upper edge, then slid down the bank to the water. "We can go over here."

Without a word, Billy sat down, trying to imitate his older friend. "Look I'm doing just like Matt!" he shouted, moments before he slipped into the sallow muddy water.

"Now look what you've done!" Jenary called out to him. "Mother's not going to like this!"

Quickly, Billy scrambled to his feet and climbed out of the creek. "I'll clean my shoes off before I get home and my clothes will dry," he said. "Mother will never know."

Jenary glanced toward heaven. "She'll know. Mother always knows."

Matt jumped over to the opposite bank, then leaned down and grabbed Billy's hand. "Let's go investigating."

Billy ran and pulled open the door to the soddy. "You're right Sis. There's no one here anymore. The claim jumpers are gone. It's empty. Hooray!"

Cobwebs hung in the corners of the room. Jenary watched a spider spin a web, then climb to the top. She thought of the mouse that ran across her bed and shuddered.

Jenary was pleased that the dugout was abandoned, and yet it seemed sad. First, Uncle John and Aunt Elizabeth had tried so hard to settle here. Now Matt and Susanne Strong and their folks had come to Elm Grove. Would they even want to live out here?

## Chapter Three
### The Indian Visit

It had been two days since Matt and Susanne had told their parents about the soddy. Jenary feared that they might not be interested in moving out of town.     After supper that night, Jenary went out to feed the chickens. Grabbing a handful of mash, she scattered it in front of the hens and rooster. Hearing the clop, clop, clop of horses and wagon wheels squeaking, Jenary turned. She threw the feed to the chickens, and hurried to the house. The wagon stopped in the yard.

Billy ran up and greeted his friend, with Spot barking. "Hi Matt!"

"Hi Susanne," Jenary said, upon reaching the wagon.

Mother emerged from the house. "Abe and Helen Strong!" she called, hurrying down the steps. "Come in the house and tell me what's happened since we left Kansas."

Mr. Strong took his missus' arm. "The children wanted us to see the dugout, but we came to visit." Abe Strong shuffled his feet. "I don't see any need to go down at the creek. Anyway, we need to get back to town before dark."

Matt jumped down then helped his sister from the wagon, then joined Billy and Spot. When her feet touched the ground Susanne hugged Jenary. "Pa said we're not going to move out here in the dugout! We're going to live in a house close to Smitty's Blacksmith Shop."

Taking her friend's hand, Jenary tried not to let her disappointment show. "I want you to live close by so we can be friends and play like we did back in Medicine Lodge."

Susanne brushed away a tear. "You will always be my best friend."

"We'll play during the school recess and we can eat together under the shade tree," Jenary assured her. "No matter what, we'll be friends."

"Like we were in Kansas," Susanne added.

"Let's go find my pa," Jenary said, tugging at her friend's hand.

Hurrying to the back yard, she saw Pa at the barn and waved to him. "We've got company."

Pa smiled at Susanne. "Did your pa and ma come?"

"They're in the kitchen drinking coffee," Jenary answered.

Pa laughed. "I'd better get inside."

Both girls flopped down on the back steps. "I wonder why your pa and ma didn't come to the Oklahoma Territory when we all came?"

"They wanted to make that run, but Grandmother got sick," Susanne said. "Really bad sick. Ma didn't want to leave her."

Jenary remembered her uncle and aunt losing their baby boy and how hard it was for Aunt Elizabeth to leave the grave. Now her uncle and aunt seemed glad to be settled in the Oklahoma Territory. She hoped that Susanne and her family would be happy here too.

"Let's go find Matt and Billy and play, "Hide and Seek," Jenary said.

Susanne shook her head. "He won't want to. Matt thinks he's too big for that 'little youngun's game.'"

Standing, Jenary reached for her friend's hand. "Let's go ask anyway."

Just then, Billy ran around the house. "I'm hiding from Matt." The sandy-haired boy jumped from behind a tree and grabbed Billy's shoulder. "I caught you!"

"Susanne and I want to play," Jenary said. "All of you can hide and I'll be 'It.'" She laid her hand against a scrub Oak tree. "Let's use this one for the base."

"Yeah," Billy shouted. "I'll bet my sis can't find us!"

With her eyes closed, Jenary heard Billy, Matt and Susanne breathing. She counted to one hundred by fives, then called out, "Ready or not, here I come."

Jenary smiled and hurried toward the bushes. She wondered who she would find first. She tiptoed up to Matt and was about to touch his shoulder.

"I'll get in free," her brother called out. He dashed across the yard in an effort to touch the Oak tree. "See!"

After everyone had a turn at being "It," Susanne ran up to Jenary. "When I was close to the barn, I heard a cat."

When Aunt Belle Master's cat had a litter, she gave Jenary a tiny black and white kitten, Callie. "I bet our Callie has had her kitten out there," Jenary replied. She ran across the yard. "Let's go see them."

Tiny meows sounded when Jenary and Susanne reached the barn. They tiptoed up to the mother cat who snuggled with her six tiny kittens in a bed of hay.      Jenary kneeled in front of Callie. "Don't get too close," she cautioned her friend. "These are her babies."

"When can I pick one up?" Susanne asked.

"When they get a little older," Jenary said. "They'll have their eyes open before too long."

Susanne clasp her hands together. "Her babies are beautiful."

Jenary felt thankful that her friend had arrived in Elm Grove. She remembered their good times back in Medicine Lodge and knew they would have fun together out here in the Oklahoma Territory. She was glad Susanne was here to share special events.

The next week, Mr. Masters explained to the class about the Cheyenne Indian Tribe and how they were moved from other states to live on reservations. He went on to describe how they tried to keep the homesteaders from taking their land.

"The Cheyenne wanted to hunt buffalo like they did when they lived in North and South Dakota," he said. "They didn't want to stay on the reservations then, but they've settled down now."

The teacher told how the Indians attempted to stop the wagons from Kansas advancing  across the border to the Territory. Jenary shivered and rubbed her arms. The wagons had crossed the border where she and her family had crossed.

After school, she and Billy walked across the pasture toward home. Jenary thought about all that she had learned about the Indians.  She hoped the Cheyenne did not go on the warpath again.

From a distance they heard a dog bark and Spot ran to meet them. Billy threw a stick. "Fetch."

Spot wagged his tail and raced after the stick. Jenary smiled. While Billy played with his dog, Jenary turned toward home, smiling at her brother and Spot antics.

Reaching the yard, Jenary was surprised to see Mother baking bread over an open fire. "It sure smells good! But why are you cooking outside?"

"I didn't want to heat up the house," Mother said. She turned the bread over on a wire grate. "Good and brown and ready to take up."

Billy slid to a stop with Spot nipping around his feet. "Can I have a piece?"

Mother smiled. "Surely you can wait until supper. We'll wait on your pa. He's plowing the north field."

Jenary craved a piece of bread also, but she knew better than to ask. Hearing the loud thunder of horses hooves, she turned to face six Indian braves riding into the yard, their ponies lathered from exertion.

The braves wore buckskin leggings, their bare chests glistened with sweat. The leader pointed at the bread and muttered words in their Indian language.

Jenary and Billy hurried to Mother. Quickly she broke the hot bread into pieces and offered some to each brave. "You take."

They mumbled, reached for the warm fragrant bread and stuffed it into their mouths.

Jenary held her breath until the red dust settled behind the imparting braves. "Thank God!"

Mother placed both hands over her face and fell onto her knees. "I thought we were goners!"

Pa hurried across the yard, stooped down and slipped his arm around Mother, Jenary and Billy. "Are you all right? They didn't hurt you, did they?"

Mother looked in Pa's face, then cried, "I was so scared!"

"I had turned the horses, ready to plow another row when I and saw those Indians ride away." Pa pulled a handkerchief out of his pocket and wiped at the dust caked sweat from his face. "I just knew they had killed my family!"

Jenary gazed at Pa. She could not remember when he had hugged them so tlghtly or when she had last seen him shed a tear.

Mr. Masters had explained in class about the Indians' hunger. At times they were near starvation.

Yet, Jenary realized that perhaps the Indian' visit had helped her family show more love for one another. "I was scared, but Mr. Masters told us that the tribes had settled. I sure hope so."

# Chapter Four
## Turkeys, Snakes and Coyotes

From the money the wheat crop brought in last spring, Pa bought a big box of groceries, more seed and something special.

Mother smiled when Pa returned from Elm Grove that September day with six poults. "Pray tell me what we are going to do with those little turkeys !"

"We'll raise them," Pa said, chuckling. He patted his tummy and Mother laughed. "Baked with stuffing, they'll taste mighty good."

"We can put them in with our chickens," Billy exclaimed. "We can see which rooster can gobble the loudest, the chicken or the turkey!"

"No, no!" Mother said. "Your Pa needs to build a pen just for the turkeys.  There were wild turkeys about, and they would lure ours away. Anyhow, they need a pen of their own. Turkeys and chickens do not get along. She smiled. "By the way, the turkey 'rooster' is called a tom."

Jenary tried to remember everything she had heard about turkeys. She had seen them on some of the farms back in Medicine Grove, but her family did not raise any. She sat down at the table. "I can feed and water the turkeys," she told Mother. "I want to learn how to take good care of them."

Jenary knew what she should do. In school tomorrow, she would ask Mr. Masters about raising turkeys.

At school the next morning, the students saluted the flag, sang a song, then said a prayer. The teacher wrote the spelling words in the corner of the black board. He opened the geography book to begin their lesson.

Jenary raised her hand. "Will you teach us about turkeys?"

Mr. Masters laughed. "It's not in our geography book, but I'll tell you everything I know."

The class clapped their hands. No geography lesson today.

"Wild turkeys are the ancestors of these domestic turkeys, the turkeys we see today," Mr. Masters said. "They roost in trees."

"Like the trees we have here?" Jake asked.

"Just like these trees," Mr. Masters replied. "The domestic turkeys like to roost about a foot above the ground."

"So they hatch from eggs like the chickens do?" Adelaide asked.

"Yes," the teacher agreed.

"Chickens and turkeys are probably cousins!" Billy announced. "Just like Kenny and Bobby are my cousins."

"Maybe so," Mr. Masters said. "Maybe so."

On her way home from school, Jenary thought about Mr. Masters' lesson about the turkeys and chickens. Later in the afternoon, she grabbed a basket off the kitchen shelf and hurried toward the hen house.

Jenary liked to take care of the chickens and now the turkeys. She laughed at the rooster strutting around the pen. She made a game out of gathering the eggs. She liked to count and see if the hens could lay more each day.

Humming, Jenary pushed the half door open and stepped inside. She shifted the basket to her left hand, then bent over the nest. "You don't mind if I take your eggs," she asked the hen.

Jenary heard a strange hiss and turned an inquisitive gaze down the row of nests. Her heart seemed to catch in her throat at the sight of the huge bull snake with a big bulge in its throat.

"AAh!" Jenary screamed. She dropped the basket as she ran out the open door. "Mother! Pa! Help! Help!"

Mother stepped out on the back porch. "What's wrong?"

"It's a big snake and he's sucking all the eggs!" Jenary shouted.

"Run and get your pa!" Mother called out.

Turning, Jenary headed for the field. From the corner of her eye, she saw the snake slithering out from under the gate. "He's coming after me! That snake is chasing me!" she cried in alarm. "Pa, come quick!"

Billy raced toward her. "What happened!"

"A snake's after me!" Jenary told him. "Go get Pa!"

Billy pointed down at his little dog. "Spot will get him for you!"

Jenary shook her head. "Better keep your dog away from that snake. He'll get the best of Spot in a hurry!"

Looking up, Jenary saw Pa running toward them.

Mother handed a hoe to Pa. "That Bull snake is mad!" She told him. "You'd better hurry!"

Pa gripped the hoe handle and hurried to the hen house. In a quick move, he slammed the blade down hard. "Got him!"

Jenary cringed, then turned around to see the snake wiggle in the red dust then lay still. "Is he dead?"

"Yes," Pa said, "the snake won't bother you anymore."

She threw herself against Pa's chest. "Thank you!"

He let the hoe slide to the ground and hugged Jenary. "That was quite a scare," he said, in a comforting voice.

Billy ran toward Pa and Jenary then pointed. "That bush is wigglng. There's another snake!"

Mother hurried  over. "They often travel in pairs."

Quickly Pa grabbed the hoe and slammed it down hard again. "That should do it!"

"I hope that's the last one." Jenary picked up the dusty basket of broken eggs and walked to the back steps. She hated to lose those eggs. Mother needed them to sell.

Jenary liked the chickens, but she did not like snakes, even the little green ones that roamed Mother's garden. There were snakes back in Medicine Lodge, but Jenary had never seen one in their hen house, or have one chase her. She shuddered every time she thought about that bull snake. She hoped she would never see another snake, ever!

At dusk, Pa and Billy went down to the barn. Jenary tailed behind them.  They heard frantic barking down by the hen house. Her brother perked up and turned toward the sound. "What's got Spot stirred up?"

"I sure hope there's not another snake bothering the chickens," Jenary said.

Pa frowned. "Not likely, at least after dark. Our chickens have had a bad day! If you ruffle the hens' feathers too much, they won't lay any eggs."

"There's Spot!" Billy dashed across the yard and down the trail.

Pa hurried after him. "I wonder what your dog's into now?"

"He's guarding our chickens! Spot's got something cornered," her brother bragged. "He's growling."

"Coyotes!" Pa called out. He grabbed Jenary's arm. "Stay here. Don't go any closer."

Billy puffed out his chest. "Spot's gonna get the best of 'em."

A thin gray coyote growled when Pa stepped in front of Jenary and Billy. "It's young," he said, "probably got separated from the pack. Spot kept him from getting our chickens."

Billy threw a rock at the coyote, and the animal turned and ran. "Get away from here!"

Pa slipped his arm around Billy's shoulder. "You and Spot saved the day."

"That was a close call," Jenary said, leaning against her pa. She wondered how else this territory could surprise them.

# Chapter Five
## The Dugout

Wet snow flakes drifted downward. It was the first snow since Jenary and her family had arrived in the Oklahoma Territory. In the early morning light, Mother stirred the pot of oatmeal, that bubbled on the iron cook stove.

Pa entered the kitchen and poured a cup of coffee. "Someone's over at that old abandoned sod house."

"At John and Elizabeth's old place?" Mother asked. "How do you know?"

Pa sipped his coffee. "One of our cows wandered over by the creek and we had to go fetch her."

Billy ran in behind Pa. "We saw foot prints in the snow. Maybe there's an outlaw or a robber hiding out!"

Jenary set bowls at each place setting. "Did you see someone in the yard?"

"Spot barked," Billy replied, "but no one came out. There

were tracks leading up to the steps."

"Perhaps the stranger's from 'No Man's Land,'" Jenary said.

"Where's that?" her brother asked.

Jenary placed the biscuits on the table. "Mr. Masters told the class about the land just west of the Cherokee Outlet. That's where all the outlaws hide out."

"Whah!" Billy shouted. "Let's get Matt and Susanne and go see it."

Mother turned away from the stove. "Now wait a minute, young man! You best forget about those robbers and such!" She stepped to Billy. "And don't you children go hanging around that old dugout."

Billy shuffled his feet. "Okay Ma."

Setting the homemade jelly out, Jenary thought about the abandoned soddy. She figured that Billy had a plan and would enlist Matt's help. Jenary did not want Billy to be in any danger. Besides that, she wanted to go along.

The next afternoon, when the last school bell rang, Jenary tramped across the snow-covered yard to meet her brother and Matt.

Pa and me saw tracks at the old dugout, "Billy called out. "Want to go and exploring?"

"Sure," Matt replied. "I need to do my chores, but that won't take long."

Susanne hurried over. "I want to go, too!"

Jenary reached for her friend's hand. "We'll go together."

Although the snow had almost melted on the school ground, it clung to Jenary's shoes as she tramped along the trail to Persimmon Creek with the explorers. Jenary wanted to know more about the stranger at the dugout.

When they climbed down the creek bank, Matt jumped

across the stream, then crawled up the wet soggy bank. Billy looked at the water, then at Matt.

"Better not try that," Jenary warned. "Your feet are already wet. Last time, you slid in and soaked your shoes."

"Jump with all your might!" Matt called out.

"How are we going to get over?" Susanne asked.

Jenary grasped Susanne's hand and together they jumped across the most shallow place of the creek. When they climbed the bank, she heard a child's voice.

A little four-year-old boy stood in front of the dugout. Jenary inched closer. "Hello."

Immediately, the front door opened and a woman stepped out onto the porch. "Come on in Raymond."

"We didn't mean to scare him," Jenary said. "We only came to see who was here."

"When did you move in?" Billy asked. "We saw the foot prints."

"I'm Lucia Gilbert." The mother pulled Raymond to her. "Those probably belonged to my husband Ethan. I need to go back in. My baby Betsy is sick."

Susanne inched closer. "What's wrong with her?"

Lucia leaned against the door. "She has a fever. She's asleep now, but Raymond and I need to see about her."

Jenary wanted to do something to help this woman. Where was the little boy's pa? "Can we come back sometime, Missus Gilbert?"

Lucia pushed a wisp of dark curly hair away from her face. "Where do you live?"

Billy stepped to the porch. "Across the creek and down the trail."

"Susanne and I live at the edge of town, behind the blacksmith shop," Matt added.

Missus Gilbert grabbed Raymond's arm and pushed him inside. "Come back again."

"We will," Jenary assured her.

After Susanne and Matt headed for home, Jenary quickly told Mother about Missus Gilbert, Raymond and the dugout. "Their little girl, Betsy is really sick."

"Perhaps you and I can go and visit them, sometime," Mother said. "We'll see if she needs help with the baby."

When Jenary came home from school the next day, she asked her mother, "Did you hear anymore more about Missus Gilbert and her children?"

Mother sat down at the table. "I made a big pot of stew. Why don't you and I walk over and take it to the needy family?"

"What about Billy?" Jenary asked.

"We better take him with us," Mother said, "otherwise there's no telling what trouble he'll get into."

That evening around the supper table, Jenary, Billy and their mother told Pa about the visit to the Gilberts' dugout.

"It seems that they came from Nebraska," Mother explained. "They were in the land race like us!" Billy said, in an excited voice.

"However they decided to settle farther east," Jenary added.

Pa sipped his coffee. "What happened?"

"Claim jumpers stole their 160 acres. Then Mr. Gilbert moved his family over this way," Mother said. "They've been camped outside of Elm Grove, but their baby got sick and they needed to keep her and Raymond warm."

Jenary scooted to the edge of the chair. "Do you think they can stay in the dugout?"

"It seems their pa went into town to register the land," Mother explained. "Lucia said that her husband was able to buy the land as a 'relinquishment' since it had been abandoned by the former owners."

"I'm glad the Gilbert family is going to be able to stay," Jenary said. "Now they have a home."

"Someday there'll be one more boy in our school," Billy announced. "Soon the boys will outnumber the girls."

Jenary laughed. "I sure hope not."

## Chapter Six
### Elm Grove's First Fair

A cool breeze rustled the gold and yellow-colored leaves, falling from the Oak and Elm trees. Standing on the back porch, Jenary wrinkled her nose at the smell of the hogs in their pen down past the barn. Shivering, she stood on tiptoes watching Minnie, the Chester-White sow lift her head, while the boar, Elmer rooted around in the mud.

Jenary remembered the day that Elmer escaped from the pig pen. That sneaky pig wandered all night. When Pa and Billy finally found Elmer, he was down by the river wallowing in the muddy water.

Billy worked to get Minnie and Elmer ready to enter the Elm Grove fair. Jenary knew they would never be able to count on Elmer to be on good behavior. He never cooperated.

Mother's entry was homemade blackberry jelly and sand plum jam. Jenary planned to enter a hand sewn pink paisley apron.

It was cut from a flour sack and Mother had helped Jenary stitch a pretty floral pattern. Her other entry was a pillow covering, made of left-over fabric from a dress she'd out grown.

At the fair on Saturday, a fellow with a fiddle played a lively tune which the musicians called a break down. Another man accompanied with a guitar. Jenary stared in amazement when she saw Adelaide strummed the guitar, playing along with them.

She knew Adelaide's uncles had taught her. Jenary did not want to play a guitar. She wished that Miss Maggie would teach her to play the piano.

Down the road from the fair was the medicine show and carnival. Jenary and Billy gasp when the bearded lady stepped out of a big tent. Minutes later a midget crawled off the back of the wagon.

It was fun to see all the other exhibits. Jenary wondered if Elmer and Minnie would win a ribbon. Billy ought to win the bluest ribbon of all, for at least keeping Elmer clean. Somehow he had persuaded Elmer to waddle by the judges instead of squealing and running away.

At the end of the day, Jenary found the table where the entries, with the ribbons, were displayed. A blue ribbon was the highest honor an entry could receive and one had been placed on Mother's blackberry jam. A red ribbon, which was second best, was on her plum jelly.

The air in Jenary seemed to swish out when she saw the ribbons adorning her entries. 'Oh my,' she thought. A blue ribbon was pinned to her pillow. Although Mother had helped arranged the different pieces of fabric, Jenary had sewn all the tiny stitches. The three judges, the town's store owners had awarded a red ribbon to Jenary's ruffled apron.

Billy ran up and grabbed Jenary's hand. "Come and look!"

he shouted, excitedly. "Come and see what happened to Elmer and Minnie! Hurry!"

Swallowing her pride, Jenary ran along beside an excited Billy. 'What had Elmer done this time?' she wondered. She had helped take care of Minnie, but managing Elmer was all Billy's job. A big smile broke across Jenary's face when the pen with the animals came into view.

"Look!" Billy pointed out. He touched the blue ribbon tacked to the pen above the boar. "Look what Elmer did!"

She could hardly believe what she saw, but Jenary gave Billy a big pat on the back. "You did the impossible!"

Pa ambled up to Billy's side. "Son, you did good," he said. He placed a firm arm around Billy's thin shoulder. "Really good."

Jenary remembered an incident after a fair in Medicine Lodge. The weather had turned really cold, before Thanksgiving when the stock was butchered. She knew what Billy was going to ask Pa today.

"Pa, please don't kill Elmer and Minnie this fall," he begged.

Sighing, Pa squeezed Billy's shoulder. "Son, you know we will need all the staples for the winter," he replied. "It will be a long cold winter."

"But Pa, what about Minnie's litter?"

"Now Son," Pa explained, in a quiet comforting voice, "you know what needs to be done."

Jenary watched Billy wipe at misty eyes, trying not to cry. She looked over at Pa and recalled how much he had changed since arriving in the Oklahoma Territory. He had become more considerate and understanding of his family. "We know, Pa."

"Thanks," Pa muttered. "I appreciate that, younguns."

At supper time, before butchering day, Mother filled the

glasses with tea. "How would you children like to go into town and spend the night with Matt and Susanne?"

Billy shuffled out of his chair ran and put his arm around Mother. "We'd like that wouldn't we Sis?"

Jenary knew the reason she and Billy were being sent into town. Pa did not want them to be at home when the hogs were killed. "Maybe I could come home later and help," Jenary suggested. "I'm not little like I was back in Kansas."

"Matt is coming out and yes, Sis, you're old enough to help," Pa said. "Billy, you can spend the day in town with Susanne and her ma. You can do Matt's chores for Missus Strong."

Billy leaned back in his chair. "I'd like that!"

Pa glanced at him. "Son, you had the biggest job getting Elmer to the fair and keeping him in the pen."

Laughing Billy took a big helping of fried potatoes. "He sure did win a big blue ribbon!"

It was settled. Jenary was going to spend the night with Susanne, then come back with Matt and Mr. Strong in the morning.

"Thanks Pa," she said. "I want to help."

After the second night freeze the annual butchering day started early.  Mother and Pa were dressed before day break. They built the fire out in back, then carried water for the big cast iron pot. Pa sharpened the three big butcher knives.

When Mr. Strong drove the team into the yard, Jenary and Matt jumped down from the wagon. Jenary glared at all of the meat lying out on the table.

She wanted so badly to ask about Elmer and Minnie, but she knew better. In life there were necessary events. She was determined to hide her disappointment from her little brother.

Hurrying over to Mother, Jenary asked, "What do you want

me to do?"

"Go inside and get more salt and brown sugar." Mother smeared the mixture onto the slabs of meat. "I need to keep going so hurry."

Minutes later, Jenary returned and poured more brown sugar and salt into the pan. "Is that enough?"

"We still need more salt," Mother said. "We want the mixture to be equal parts of both, Honey."

Looking over, Jenary watched Pa dragging the large black cast iron kettle across the yard. Mr. Strong and Mr. Masters hurried to help. They placed it over the fire, then poured water into the kettle. Missus Masters and Mother threw bits of meat into the pot.

Pa grabbed an old broom handle and stirred. "Can I do that?" Jenary asked.

"The fire's too hot, Sis. Let me do this," Pa said, giving the meat another stir. "You can help with the cracklings."

Little by little the meat was brought into the kitchen, and Mother cut it into chops, roast and hams. Jenary carefully trimmed the pieces to grind into sausage. "This will sure taste good this winter," Jenary said, trying to act more grown up.

Smiling, Mother continued working. "It sure will Honey."

Jenary thought this was the longest day she had ever known. It felt as if Prince and Sadie had walked across her back, and her feet hurt something fierce.

Even though she was exhausted, Jenary felt proud of helping Mother and Pa prepare a winter's supply of meat. Jenary looked everything they had achieved. "We're almost done."

After the work was finished, Pa shook Mr. Masters hand. "Thank you." With an offer of salted meat, Pa said. "Call when you need my help."

"You're mighty welcome!" Fred masters said. "We'd better get on home. There's still chores to do before dark."

Mr. Strong and Matt climbed into their wagon. Pa reached up and shook Abe's hand. "I appreciate everything you've done. I'm especially grateful to your missus for letting Billy stay at your place today." Then Pa laughed. "My son's not quite as big as he thinks he is."

"We're just glad we were here to help," Abe Strong said. He looked toward the horses. "Giddyup."

Jenary stayed in the kitchen, helping Mother fix supper while Pa went to town to retrieve Billy. She knew that her brother would pester Pa all the way home. Not until they had sat down for supper would Billy ask about Elmer and Minnie.

While pretending to look down at her plate, Jenary peeked at Billy. She cringed when tears formed at the corner of her brother's eyes.

"What happened to Elmer and Minnie?"

Pa reached over and laid a consoling hand on Billy's arm. "We had enough meat so we saved those pigs so you can spoil them," he said, smiling. "Maybe Minnie will give us a big litter of pigs again next year."

Leaping up from the table, Billy wrapped his arms around their Pa's neck. "Oh thank you, Pa! Thank you."

Although she had dared not ask about Minnie and Elmer, Jenary was thankful that Pa had saved the sow and boar for Billy to tend.

Her birthday would soon be here. She and Billy both had something to celebrate.

## Chapter Seven
### The Birthday Party

In late October,  the Elm and Oak Tree leaves were turning a gorgeous red and golden yellow leaves had fallen limply to the ground. The evening sun had sunk  below the stark prairie, sent shafts of sunlight through the naked trees.

The cool breeze drifted through the trees and touched Jenary's  cheeks. With the arithmetic  tucked under her arm, she crossed the pasture and hurried toward home.

She could not believe they had been in the Oklahoma Territory more than a year. Her family had been living in the soddy when she turned twelve years old. Jenary would have her thirteen birthday next week. She knew that Mother would bake a birthday cake if she could find the fixings.

"Better go get the eggs and feed the chickens, Mother said. "Billy's out helping your pa milk the cows."

Later, at the supper table Billy stuffed his mouth with fried potatoes, while lecturing about farming. "Pa, in geography class, Miss Maggie said that you should plant hard red winter wheat. That's what they planted in Illinois."

"Your teacher's right son," Pa said. "It grows better in this part of the country. This year you can help me with the planting."

Billy continued eating. "The teacher said that we need to get the seeds into the ground before the first freeze."

"We'll do that," Pa assured him.

Jenary smiled. Since another classroom was added to the school house, the younger children had  moved into it. She had not been sure if Billy would be willing to stay in a room apart from her. Yet he listened and learned well. "Miss Maggie is a good teacher."

"She sure is," Billy agreed. "She said that in the spring we can put our cows on the wheat and let them eat."

Pa pushed his plate away. "Our herd is growing. The new crop will feed them until they have their calves."

"Then the  winter wheat will begin to grow again," Billy said, eagerly. "We need to plant our wheat about 2 or 3 inches deep, but it can't live, if it's sitting in a lot of water."

Pa sipped his coffee. "I'm proud of you, son. You've done a fine job learning all about crops."

"I'll be a big help to you, won't I, Pa?" Billy asked.

Patting his son's arm, Pa said. "You're already a big help, but now you've learned more about farming, you can help me even more."

Billy puffed out his chest.  "I'll work with you in the field and Jenary can take care of those awful ole turkeys. They pecked at Spot and me again. We don't like them."

Pa laughed. "You'll be a farmer yet. Maybe we'll cook one of those ornery birds for Thanksgiving."

"I want the drumstick," Billy insisted, smacking his lips.

Jenary liked the turkeys. She enjoyed watching their big feathers fold at night when they went to roost. "Billy, you need to stay away from them," she scolded. You aggravate them.

When Jenary arrived home the next afternoon, Mother met her at the door. "I've cooked a big pot of soup and intended to take it over to the Gilbert's place, but Pa needs more wheat and wants to go into town. I have some eggs so I'll go along."

"I'll take the soup over to Missus Gilbert," Jenary assured. "I can feed the chickens when I get back."

Mother tied her bonnet. "I'll tell Billy that he needs to help you with your chores."

After waving good-bye, Jenary hurried down the trail. The pot was heavy, but she switched hands. She looked for the most shallow place, then stepped across the creek, walked to the dugout, and knocked on the door.

Missus Gilbert opened the door, then stood wringing her hands nervously."Betsy and I are here," she said, "but Raymond is gone."

"What happened to your little boy?"

"He's been cooped up inside and begged to play outside," Missus Gilbert said, "So I told him that he could go outside for a little while."

"Maybe he wandered off," she soothed.

Tears slid down Missus Gilbert's cheeks. "I called out for Raymond, but the baby's been sick and I couldn't leave to look for him. He likes to look at the creek, but I warned him to stay away from the edge."

Jenary handed the pot to the woman. "Mother sent the soup over for your little girl."

The frantic mother brushed at the tears. "Thank you," she whispered, reaching for the pot handle.

"I'll find Raymond," Jenary said, then turned away, looking beyond the clearing. Where could the little boy have gone? She hoped he had fallen into the creek like Billy had done.

She ran behind the dugout and down the trail, looking all around for the four-year-old. Jenary hurried up the incline, then turned and stare over the edge of the cliff. "Oh no," she called out. At the bottom of the ravine, lay Raymond.

Pulling her coat tightly around her, Jenary slid down the hill. She kneeled beside the boy and touched his cold cheek. "Wake up," she whispered. Raymond did not open his eyes.

Leaning down close to his mouth, Jenary saw his faint warm breath in the cold crisp air. 'He's alive, but how am I going to get him up that hill?'

"Sis, where are you?"

Startled, Jenary looked up. "Billy is that you?"

"Yeap. Spot and I have been looking everywhere for you."

"Raymond's fallen down the hill," she told her brother, "and I can't get him out. You need to run and get some help."

Billy turned on his heel. "I'll run to Uncle Fred's house. He'll help!"

"All right, but hurry! We don't want anything to happen to Raymond!"

Jenary rubbed the little boy's hand. 'The wind was knocked out of him.'

She closed her eyes in silent prayer. 'Please don't let him be hurt really bad.'

Raymond opened weary eyes and tried to get to his feet. "I want my ma."

At that moment, Jenary thought she had never heard anything sweeter than Raymond's sobs. "I'll take you home," she whispered, "as soon as my brother brings help. Remember Billy?"

The little boy smiled. "Yes."

Although it seemed like a hour since her brother left, Jenary heard footsteps at the top of the ravine and looked up. "Billy."

"Hey Sis, I brought someone to help us."

Glancing up, Jenary caught her breath. Two Indians stood beside her brother. "Oh!"

"Look at the scar on his cheek," Billy said, proudly gesturing to the Indian. "These are the braves that came to our house."

"And Mother gave them hot bread," Jenary added. "Are you going to help us?"

One of the Indians climbed down and picked Raymond up in his arms. "Not big."

"We'd better hurry," she said. "The little boy's Mother is worried sick."

At the edge of the yard, the brave set Raymond down, then hurried to the trees.

Jenary touched the little boy's arm. "You can walk from here."

"Thank you, "Missus Gilbert whispered. Through tears streaming down her face, she smiled. "Thank you very much."

Jenary was thankful they were able to return Raymond to his mother. It was the first time she had seen her neighbor smile. "I'm thankful we found him."

After a good night's sleep, she felt better the next morning. That afternoon Jenary tossed a hand full of feed out to the chickens. She laughed at the strutting Dominique rooster with his long tail feathers that drooped to the ground.

After supper, she lowered the bucket down into the water in the well. Pa used old bits and pieces of lumber from what the tornado left of the lean-to shelter to build an encasement around the well. Finally he positioned  a pulley over the opening.

Jenary yanked on the rope and pulled up the heavy bucket. With water sloshing against her leg, she hurried home. In the twilight she admired the porch Pa had built across the front of the house.

She remembered helping her mother plant zinnia and four-o'clock seeds that they had brought from Kansas. They found a wild rose and a small lilac bush down by Persimmon Creek. With Pa's shovel, she and Mother dug them up and replanted them close to the house. Although the run-away herd had trampled them, now they both were growing and the rose bush was already blooming.

The bushes had given off such a sweet fragrance in the spring.  Mother promised that they would plant a red trumpet honey suckle vine beside the posts on the porch. Hummingbirds loved the Yellow and Pink blooms.

Lying in bed that night, Jenary pulled the quilt up to her neck. She liked talking and planning for Thanksgiving, but what about her birthday? Had Pa and Mother have forgotten?

The next morning the air was chilly and crisp. Jenery's breath came out like puffs of smoke when she walked toward school in Elm Grove. She could not believe that her special day had arrived.

No one mentioned her birthday that morning at school. At noontime buckets were opened and sausage and biscuits were eaten, when her friend glanced over at Jenary.

"Happy birthday," Susanne announced said, placing a hand on Jenary's pail.

Adelaide nibbled on a biscuit. "How old are you?"

"Thirteen," Jenary replied, thankful that her friends had

remembered her birthday. Neither Pa or Mother had said anything. Was she going to have a birthday cake?

Trying to hide her disappointment that afternoon, Jenary focused on her arithmetic problems. The class was studying fractions. By the time the last bell rang, Jenary could hardly bring herself to walk out the door of the school. However when she looked at the road in front of the building, there stood their wagon filled with hay. Pa sat on his seat chuckling. "Surprise!"

Jenary put her hand over her mouth. Everyone in class ran toward the wagon and climbed aboard. "Happy birthday," Mr. Reynolds called out. He climbed onto the hay and sat down beside Miss Maggie.

Pa smiled. He held the reins lightly, yet Prince and Sadie stamped anxiously. "Did you think that we had forgotten your birthday?"

Tears clouded Jenary's eyes, but she blinked them back. "I didn't know."

"We worked really hard to keep our plans a secret," Billy said. "Did we really surprise you, Sis?"

"You fooled me!" she replied.

"Giddyup, Prince," Pa called out. "Giddyup, Sadie."

When the wagon started down the road, Miss Maggie lead the children in the birthday song. "Happy birthday to you. Happy birthday to you. Happy birthday, dear Jenary , happy birthday to you!"

Billy threw a handful of hay into Mr. Master's hair. "Watch out there," the school teacher called out in a good natured way.

Jenary realized that the wagon was headed toward their farm. What had Mother and Pa planned?

When the team stopped in the yard, Mother rushed out to

greet everyone. "Come on in."

Jenary felt special when the boys helped the girls down. Matt took her hand. "Come on, Birthday girl."

After he let go of her hand, Jenary saw him lift the horses hooves, inspecting them. "My brother's been hanging around the blacksmith shop," Susanne said, softly. "He thinks he might want to learn to be a smitty."

Mother had baked a two-layered white cake, placed it on a milk glass platter, and frosted the cake with a white creamy mixture. To Jenary, her birthday cake looked like a huge snowball.

After her classmates sang 'Happy Birthday' again, Jenary sliced a piece of cake for Miss Maggie and one for Mr. Reynolds. Mother served glasses of tea, while Jenary cut bigger pieces for all of the girls.

"The boys want some, too." Billy protested.

Pa laid his hand on his son's shoulder. "Hold your horses. Ladies first."

Smiling, Jenary then made sure everyone had a piece of cake. This was the best birthday since she and her family had moved to the Oklahoma Territory.

# Chapter Eight
## Thanksgiving

Jenary jumped out of bed and hurried to the kitchen. She looked through the glass window. With the back of her hand, she rubbed the steam off the pane.

A Blanket of soft white snow covered the bushes, young trees and stumps still in the ground. The snowflakes shimmered in the early morning light.

Barefooted, Billy ran and pulled the back door open. "It looks like Christmas!" He stuck a big toe into the snow. Spot scampered past him, then screeched to an abrupt stop. "Go on out," he told the dog, giving him a big push of encouragement. Spot lunged forward and the snow nearly buried him.

Mother tugged at Billy's shirt. "Well, it's not Christmas and shut the door young man," she scolded. "We're all freezing!"

Pa sat at the table drinking coffee. "Son, the snow's deep, so it'll take us longer to care for the animals. Now you'd better get your clothes on so we can go feed the cattle."

"In just a minute, Billy replied. He opened the door again and Spot dashed in, shaking snow all over the floor.

"When I finish this cup and pull on my coat, you and your dog had been be ready."

Jenary attempted to hide a smile. It seemed that Pa and Billy had this conversation every morning. She wanted to admonish her brother to hurry, but

she knew that Spot gave Billy enough trouble.

Dragging his feet, Billy trudged to the back room and struggled into his socks and scuffed high top shoes. Spot jumped and nipped at the strings. "Stop that," Billy scolded, "you ornery dog. Pa'll leave us behind."

When they closed the back door, her mother turned toward Jenary. "Let's get breakfast ready. Pa and Billy will be starving when they come in."

"Mother, can you remember when we had this much snow just before Thanksgiving?"

"Yes," she said. "We were back in Kansas. You were little and you may not remember when we had snow for Thanksgiving and Christmas."

"I want the snow to go away before Thanksgiving," Jenary said. "If it's like this, Sarah and the little boys can't come for dinner."

Shoving the biscuits into the oven, Mother sprinkled flour into the skillet. "Honey in this Oklahoma Territory I've learned one thing. "It can snow and be bad for a day or so, then a few days later, the snow will be gone."

"I hope it's that way this year," Jenary said. If it isn't snowing or raining, maybe everyone can come for our Thanksgiving dinner!"

"One of the yearlings is missing!" Billy shouted, when he sat down at the table for breakfast.

"Is that true?" Mother asked. "One of our calves is gone."

"I'm afraid so," Pa said, spooning gravy over his biscuits. "There's marks in the snow, but I can't tell what happened."

"A coyote probably dragged it away," Billy said, eating his biscuits and gravy.

"Or it could be Indians," Pa muttered.

Jenary stared down at her plate. Her pa seemed to have changed and now this outburst. Would he never understand and accept the Indians?

Don't be that way, Will," Mother scolded. "Look what they did for the little Gilbert boy."

"Pa, he wasn't moving ," Jenary said. "If it hadn't been for the Indians' help, Billy and I would never been able to get the boy out of the ravine."

Sipping from a glass of milk, Billy looked over at Mother. "Can Spot and I play in the snow?"

Their mother shook her head. "You'll come in all wet and dirty. Everything will be. . . "

Pa walked over and slipped his arm around his wife's waist. "Oh let the young'uns have a little fun."

"I want to go too!" Jenary called out.

"Okay," Mother said, laughing. "Remember you need to wear those coats to school tomorrow."

After school the next day, Jenary went with Billy to feed the herd, while Pa finished with the other chores.

"Look," Billy shouted. A familiar scar-faced Indian pulled an arrow out of a fallen coyote. Nearby lay the remains of the missing yearling.

Jenary stepped closer to her brother."It's probably the same coyote that was after our chickens."

"Our Indian friend stopped it from getting any more of our herd!" Billy exclaimed.

She watched the Indian place the arrow into a leather pouch, then pick up the fallen yearling and sling it over his back. "He wants to take the calf, but what will Pa say?"

"He'll probably be glad the coyote is dead," Billy said.

"I hope he doesn't get mad about this," Jenary whispered.

After supper, the week before Thanksgiving, Pa frowned, then laid his arm on Billy's shoulder. "You should have come and got me when you found the dead yearling."

"There wasn't time," Billy said.

Gripping Billy's shoulder tighter, Pa asked. "Did you even try to stop him from taking the calf away?"

"If he hadn't stopped the coyote, it would have killed some of the cows too," Jenary added.

"I just hate to lose the yearling," Pa said, softly. "Perhaps his family is hungry, even starving. I know you children did the best you could. I'm proud of you."

Jenary clasped her hands together. She knew her brother was glad Pa understood about the yearling and the Indians' plight. She prayed silently. 'Their pa was gradually changing!'

Thanksgiving week at the supper table Mother sipped a glass a glass of ice tea. "We ought to plan our Thanksgiving dinner. I wonder if John and Elizabeth and the children can come."

"Let' ask Matt and Susanne and their folks," Billy added.

"That's a good idea," Mother agreed. "Maybe they can invite Smitty to accompany them. Since his wife died, the Strongs try to include him in their doings."

The day before Thanksgiving, Pa selected a turkey out of

the flock. He killed it , plucked the feathers, then brought it into the kitchen. For a week, Mother had been saving the left over cornbread. "I want to make a big batch of dressing," she said. "That Tom turkey is huge."

Early on Thanksgiving morning, Jenary listened to the pans chime through the open kitchen window. She glanced out the bedroom window at the north western sky, hovering in darkness. Mother was already up preparing the feast.

Rubbing her eyes, Jenary pushed back the quilt and touched her feet to the cold floor. Mother had cooked pies and cakes before she went to bed last evening. She had made a pumpkin, apple and mincement pie, then cooked a chocolate cake and a blackberry cobbler.

Sunlight peeked above the horizon when Jenary entered the kitchen. Pouring herself a glass of milk, she broke open a biscuit and spread a dab of butter between the halves.

Pa slammed the back door and stomped his feet. "Smells good in here," he said, pouring a cup of coffee. He gazed at the row of baked goods on the counter.

"Mother's been busy," Jenary said. "I've been helping her. I'm learning to make pie crust, but she did all of these."

"You're doing awful well Sis," he said, in a proud voice.

Pa stared at the turkey. "That's one of the largest birds that I've ever seen. Look how it hangs over the edge of the baking pan."

Slipping his arm around Mother, Pa said. "It's a good thing the turkey is so big. As hard working folks, we'll probably eat all of it."

Smiling, Jenary nibbled on her biscuit. Pa was noticing and complimenting Mother more frequently. Coming to this Oklahoma Territory had helped in many ways.

When Billy stumbled into the kitchen, Pa poured a cup of cold water into the wash pan. "Come and wash your face Son. We need to go feed the cattle."

"Aw Pa," Billy grumbled. "It's Thanksgiving!"

"Don't you think the cows get hungry on a holiday?" Pa asked.

"Yes, but . . . ."

"But nothing. Let's go," Pa laughed, "or we'll miss the Thanksgiving dinner."

Jenary peeled potatoes, then put them in a pan and set them on the stove to cook. She helped Mother open jars of green beans, corn, and black eye peas.

"Can I help you stuff the turkey," Jenary asked.

Mother tore into the pieces of cornbread and placed them in a big pan. "Let's get all the ingredients for the dressing, ready to mix together."

After Jenary placed the onions, eggs and, spices on the table, she asked. "Who is coming to our Thanksgiving dinner?"

While Mother broke the eggs into a bowl, Jenary added the sage seasoning, then sprinkled in salt and pepper. "Let's see," Mother began, "Your Uncle John and Aunt Elizabeth and their family. Abe and Ellen Strong agreed to come along with Smitty."

"If Sarah helps Aunt Elizabeth get Kenny and Bobby dressed," Jenary said, "maybe they'll be here before too long."

Laughter filled the room. Happily Mother stirred the onions into the mixture. "I've invited the Gilberts to have Thanksgiving dinner with us. Lucia agreed to come if Betsy gets well."

"There'll be a house full," Jenary assured her mother," but we'll have a good time."

"Yes we will," Pa said, stepping into the warm kitchen.

Billy slid across the kitchen floor. "Remember, the drumstick is mine!"

While she was arranging the plates and silverware on the table, a knock sounded at the front door. Jenary hurried to answer it. There stood two Indians.

"Happy Thanksgiving" she said, in greeting.

The scar-faced Indian shoved a pair of moccasins into Jenary's hands. "You!"

"Thank you," she said. She knew that he probably made these from the hide of the yearling he took.

Pa stepped forward. "We appreciate your help."

The scar-faced Indian nodded.

Mother walked to the door. "Won't you stay?" she asked, opening the door wider.

Jenary looked at the younger Indian. Just then he placed a foot over the threshold, but the older Indian shook his head.

"They won't eat Thanksgiving dinner with us," Jenary said. "Mr. Masters told us that some of the Indians became friendly, but they still distrust most of the white people."

Mother hurried to the door again with two thick slices of hot bread and pieces of pies. She held the food out the braves. "You take some of dinner with you."

The two Indians reached for the food, then the scar-faced brave nodded before both turned and ran across the snow.

'What a Thanksgiving' Jenary thought. However she was so very thankful that Pa had thanked the Indians for their help.

Mother stood at the stove, white faced. "What a scare!"

"They were kind and gave Jenary the pretty moccasins," Billy said.

Pa said, "Our company would never believe our tale."

"It's almost time for everyone to come," Mother said, still a bit nervous.

Billy pulled back the curtain and pushed his nose up to the glass. He jumped when he heard the knock on the door. He dropped the curtain and hurried to answer it.

"Come on in, Aunt Elizabeth," Jenary said, reaching for Kenny's hand.

"Hello," her cousin said. Sarah held tightly onto Bobby, even though he squirmed to break loose.

Elizabeth hurried to the kitchen with a big bowl of sweet potatoes. "There's enough here to feed an army!" she said, laughing. "What else needs to be done?"

By the time Mother had put more rolls into the oven and placed the browned turkey on a big platter, more guests had arrived. Jenary hurried to open the door for Abe Strong, the missus, Matt and Susanne. "Happy Thanksgiving. Come on in."

Smitty followed the family into the house. "I'm much obliged to you folks for inviting me," Mr. Smith said, humbled by the warm greeting.

After Pa, Uncle John and Billy came to the kitchen, Billy said, "I'm hungry."

"Smells good," Pa added.

There was a knock on the back door. Mr. Gilbert pulled open the door. "Your missus invited us." He held on to Raymond's hand.

"I've some fixings," Lucia said. She moved beside her husband, Ethan. "We don't want to impose."

"Nonsense," Pa said, "you're mighty welcome to our home!"

While the children played, the women folks placed the spread of food on the table.

Mother announced. "Before we eat, we'll go around the

table and everyone share at least one thing they're thankful for."

Jenary remembered last Thanksgiving and how they ate dinner at Uncle Fred and Aunt Belle's house. She felt grateful that her family and friends could be together for dinner.

Kenny and Bobby were walking and getting into everything. Jenary's heart was filled to overflowing with thankfulness.

# Chapter Nine
## Christmas

December arrived in full force with a cold north wind and blowing Snow.

That morning, Pa and Billy trudged to the barn to feed the herd and do the morning chores.

Billy shivered, then backed up to the fire."I thought the milk would freeze before it hit the bucket!"

"Let's sit down and thank God for his blessings," Mother said.

Billy shoved a bite of biscuit and gravy into his mouth. "My toes are still cold!"

"It's pretty cold out there," Pa said, chuckled.

After Jenary dipped the dishes into the hot, soapy water, Mother said. "This is Saturday morning and since we can't go outside, I want to open the gallon jar of
wild grapes."

Turning back around, Jenary said. "Are we going to make jelly?"

"Yes," Mother said. "I managed to save some extra sugar and we need to get these done while we have the time."

Jenary smiled. She knew her mother planned to give those jars of jelly for Christmas gifts.

After breakfast Mother poured more coffee, then sat down at the table for a brief moment. She glanced at Pa. "Would you please move my sewing machine in the back room ?" she asked. "There I can get all of the daylight."

Pa looked over at Mother. "Will it be warm enough in there?" he asked.

"If Billy will keep the fire going and if I leave the bedroom door open, the room will stay warm."

"Billy and I will move it. Won't we son?" Pa asked. "And he will keep the fire going, won't you?"

"Yes, Pa."

The look that Pa gave her brother brooked no quarrel. Mother was sewing special gifts for Christmas, but Jenary knew better than to ask questions.

The cold north wind blew hard and snow hung on every bush and tree on the way to school. It was bitter cold, but Mr. Masters built a fire that warmed the classroom.

Jenary and the other students cut out Christmas bells and stars. They took turns using the colored pencils. Mr. Masters and Miss Reynolds hung every bell and star around the school room.

That night at supper, Jenary ate the last bit of pinto beans and cornbread. "Mr. Masters said that we might go out and find a tree to decorate."

Pa sipped his coffee. "I reckon he'll have lots to choose

from."

"I hope that my teacher lets us get a tree," Billy said, excitedly.

"We'll probably have only one big tree for all the school," Jenary added.

Last Christmas, the sun had shined brightly. It had not been Christmas enough for Jenary. Back in Kansas the trees had been covered with snow.

"When can we go find our Christmas tree?" Billy asked.

"We want to decorate it," Jenary said, "like we did back in Medicine Lodge."

Jenary remembered how they had popped corn, strung it on Mother's sewing thread, then draped the strands over the tree. She hoped they could have a tree like that one. "Mother, remember when Billy and I cut out a bell?" she asked. "We used it for a pattern to make bell cookies."

Mother laughed. "Yes. We spent most of the afternoon, but they were just beautiful!"

Jenary knew Billy had the same memories ."They were big cookies," Billy said, excitedly.

"They were pretty and tasted good," Jenary added. "May we make Christmas cookies again?"

"Your Mother doesn't have time for all of that this year," Pa said, in mock dismay. "She has chores . . . ."

"We'll help Mother do her chores," Billy interrupted.

Jenary watched Pa attempt to hide a smile behind his hand. Pa always enjoyed Christmas along with the rest of the family.

The next Monday, Mr. Masters carried a big wooden box, filled with Christmas decorations, into the school room.

"Can we see them?" the little first grader Jessee asked,

peeking into the box of carefully wrapped treasures.

Jenary wanted to see the decorations also, but she stood back while the younger children gathered around. "How pretty" she sighed, when Miss Maggie unwrapped a red glass bell. Jenary longed to touch the fine decorations.

Each morning, all the students met together to salute the flag, then repeat the Lord's prayer, and sing. Miss Maggie stood beside the piano.

"Would like to sing a Christmas carol?"

When the students joined in with a huge 'yes,' Jenary glanced over at Susanne and smiled. She wondered if her friend recalled the Christmas program and the songs the class sang back in Medicine Lodge.

The melody of "Little Town Of Bethlehem," filled the room. After that carol, Miss Maggie played, "Away In The Manager."

The teacher encouraged the students, "Let's all sing."

Warmth filled Jenary's heart. She could not wait to go tell Mother about the Christmas decorations. How Jenary enjoyed singing, especially when Miss Maggie played Christmas carols. "Silent Night, holy night, . . . " Jenary whispered.

She had often wondered where the piano came from. One day she overheard Mr. Masters tell Pa that Miss Maggie brought her piano all the way from Illinois. The teacher had kept the secret, but now Jenary knew the answer.

The north wind blew and wet snow clung to the trees. When the recess bell rang, Jenary pulled on her coat, boots and mittens and went outside.

Billy inched closer to Matt. "Let's ask our teachers if we can make snow ice cream!"

"Won't that be fun! I bet they'll help us." Jenary said.

"Yum. That will taste good," Susanne agreed.

Later Mr. Masters said. "It's a great idea! Let's do that tomorrow."

Walking home after school, Jenary thought about the last winter back in Kansas. The teacher had brought milk and all of the fixings for the special treat. Jenary hoped the students at 'Rockford School' could make ice cream.

The next morning, Miss Maggie handed the big cast iron pot to Mr. Masters.  "Some of the children can help you and we'll make ice cream."

Billy, Jared and Jake cried out. "Yea!"

"We want to go with you," Jessee and Sarah said, in unison.

Jenary hurried after the little girl with a scarf and quickly wrapped it around her head. "There. Now you won't catch cold."

Back inside the school building Miss Maggie stirred the mixture of milk and sugar. Jenary dribbled a cap full of vanilla into the pan. "How's that.

"Just right," Miss Maggie replied.

Matt and Justin set the pot on the teacher's desk. "Let's add the snow," she instructed.

Miss Maggie placed the lid back on the pot. "The fellows can take this outside now."

"Okay," Mr. Master's said. "We'll bring back the ice cream."

"Yeah," Jake called out. "How long until we have ice cream?"

"Soon," Mr. Masters replied. "We'll check to see if it's freezing hard."

After what seemed like forever, Matt and Justin carried the pan inside. Miss Maggie dipped ice cream into each student's bowl. "This is the best ice cream I've ever tasted," Billy said, between bites. Jenary agreed.

The class had fun with snow. Later they would sing Christmas carols just like Miss Maggie promised.

With a cold north wind blowing, Jenary hoped they would have more snow. She longed for a white Christmas. She planned to give presents to Pa and Mother, but what gift could she give to her mischievous brother?

After suppertime on Christmas eve, Pa brought in his ax, then he, Billy and Jenary went down to the creek to hunt for a tree.

"We want it to reach the ceiling!"

Jenary clasp her hands together. "We'll make decorations and everything."

"Let's look for a cedar that's not too big," Pa explained, chuckling. "We don't want to lose the roof to our house."

After Pa chopped down the tree, Jenary helped drag the cedar home. "It will look pretty when we get all the bulbs and bells on it."

"How will it stand up?" Billy asked, excitely.

"Watch how I do this," Pa said. "That's how you'll learn."

Pa nailed two boards together in an "X", then tacked the base onto the stand. When the tree was upright in the front room, Mother took down a wooden box from the bedroom shelf. She set it down beside the tree, then pulled open the lid.

"It's Christmas ornaments!" Jenary called out. She reached for a star, then the bell. "We've had these ever since I can remember."

"They're keepsakes from your grandma," Mother said. "She gave them to your pa and me the first Christmas that we were married."

Later, Mother placed a spoon full of lard into the cast iron skillet, then poured in the hard dry corn. She moved the skillet back and forth over the fire until the kernels of corn hit the lid. Soon, the skillet was filled with white, fluffy corn.

Jenary and Billy cut strips of paper, then colored them with special colored pencils. To make paste she placed a spoon full of flour on a saucer, added a drop of water and stirred it briskly. "Let's paste these strips together, then we'll make chains and hang them on the Christmas tree."

After they cut stars and bells of paper, Mother brought a needle to the front room. "I'll make a hole in the popcorn, put the thread through them, then you can hang the strands on the tree."

At the dinner table, Mother drank a glass of tea. "Reverend Cooper is holding Christmas eve services tonight. I want the family to attend."

"When can we open the presents?" Billy asked, excitedly.

Mother laughed. "On Christmas morning, like we do every year."

At the church, Jenary glanced at the assembled crowd. Close to the front sat Sarah, Matt and their parents. On the last row Lucia Gilbert, with little Betsy in her arms, sat beside Ethan and Raymond. The whole community seemed to be present.

"Silent night, Holy night . . . ." the congregation sang.

At the close of the service, the minister said a prayer. "Thank you dear God for all of the blessings you've given us this year. In His name, Amen."

Lying in bed that night, Jenary closed her eyes, but lay awake and wondered about the presents under the tree. She really hoped her brother liked his gift.

Early the next morning, Billy rushed in to her room. "Hurry and get up!"

Jenary rubbed her eyes, pushed back the covers, then touched her feet to the floor. "Brrr," she muttered. "It's freezing in here!"

Billy ran to the door. "Let's go!"

Mother had sewn a pink flannel gown with a matching robe for Jenary. "It's pretty," she said. "really pretty."

Billy tore open a package. "A pair of men's work boots. I can lace them up. They're just like the ones the soldiers from Camp Supply wore!"

When Billy opened his gift from Jenary, he took out the leather collar and asked, "For me or Spot?"

Laughing, Mother wiped at her eyes, then said, "It's for your dog, but after some of your antics, it may fit you."

Jenary smiled. She knew Mother and Pa planned carefully for her and Billy's gifts. She had sewn the gown and robe with loving care. Somehow they had managed to get the 'grownup boots' for Billy. Jenary was glad Smitty had made the collar especially for Spot.

After the paper and sacks were cleaned up around the tree, Jenary helped Mother cook breakfast, wash and dry the dishes and put them away. She glanced at the counter, covered with cherry and apples pies and plum pudding.

"The ham is in the oven," Mother said. "We'll put in some sweet potatoes in a little while."

Outside snow piled up against the window. Jenary was thankful for the warmth inside the house.

"I'm thankful that we built our home in the Oklahoma Territory. We've laughed and been happier here than we were back in Kansas."

"At times I thought we'd better pack up and go back to a tamer land," Mother said.

"We've come too far to give up now," Pa replied.

He had persuaded Mother to join in the land rush and make

their home in Oklahoma Territory. Although the family lived in a soddy, neighbors helped Pa build a new house.

Jenary was glad when the church and school were built in Elm Grove. She enjoyed learning about the Indians, how they lived in the territory and even their hardships.

A warmth swept over Jenary's heart. This was their home. With Matt and Billy's help, she felt certain that she and Susanne would have many more adventures in this Oklahoma Territory.

## THE END

9 781947 191280